Dedication

This book is dedicated to:

The Lord God Almighty Himself
who has ...
carried me,
comforted me,
guided me,
and forgiven me ~
countless times.

And to:

Staff Sgt. Brandon Forrest Eggleston who died April 26, 2012,
in Ghazni province, Afghanistan, from injuries sustained when
his team's vehicle encountered an improvised explosive
device. He was assigned to 4th Battalion, 3rd Special Forces
Group, Fort Bragg, N.C. In addition to decorations already
received, Staff Sgt. Eggleston was posthumously awarded
several more, including the Purple Heart,
Bronze Star Medal and Combat Infantry Badge.
He was 29 and is survived by his wife, Karen, and two
daughters, 4 and 1.

*Greater love has no one than this, that he lay down his life for
his friends.* ~ John 15:13

Joanne M. Anderson, author

~ ~ ~ ~

Your word is a lamp to my feet and a light for my path.
Psalm 119:105

A portion of book and Noble Spirit Horse Club profits is donated quarterly
to therapeutic riding and equine rescue organizations.
This information is posted to the Web site:
www.anoblespirit.com

Library of Congress Control Number: 2012904259

ISBN 978-0-9706542-1-2

Book cover and interior design by Country Media, Inc. ~ Blacksburg, Virginia

Printed in the U.S.A.
by Morris Publishing®
3212 E. Hwy 30 | Kearney, NE 68847
800-650-7888 | www.morrispublishing.com

Acknowledgements

Writing and publishing a book takes time and energy, and, in my case, a few good friends. Some offered listening ears and words of encouragement over cups of tea. Others read the story at various stages of completion and offered feedback. Still more checked facts and proofread copy.

My early reader pals include close horse friend Diane Coleman, who also permitted her gorgeous, white Arabian, Kazi, to be one of the real horses in the book. Professional writer Rachael Garrity, along with Liz Albitz, Larry Kyle and Deb Schug, read the manuscript and offered suggestions. Dr. Rebecca Young, Noble and Cash's veterinarian and owner of Cedar Run Equine and Veterinary Services, provided her expertise. Chris Faith, elder at Blacksburg Christian Fellowship and former missionary to Spain (handy for checking accuracy of a few Spanish phrases), took on a reading. Friend and former ER physician, Dr. Jim Stone, kindly offered his medical perspective.

A special thanks goes to Karen Eggleston, mother of two small children and wife to Staff Sergeant Brandon Eggleston. At the time of her reading and checking facts, they were stationed at Fort Bragg, N.C., and Brandon was serving in Afghanistan. Bob Klein, Ex-Army friend, also assisted.

My special friend and riding buddy, Summer Driscoll, read the book and helped with the Noble Spirit Horse Club concept and reality. She also allowed Paloosa, her amazing Appaloosa, to participate in "A Noble Spirit" and book signings

My colleague Phillip Vaught, president of Country Media, Inc., has been invaluable with his talent and expertise. He and his staff laid out the book, managed the interior design, and created the cover design, the Noble Spirit Horse Club logo and other Noble Spirit graphics and posters.

My wonderful horse life would not be possible without the ongoing kindness and generosity of the Whittiers and loving support of my husband, John Eric Anderson. Thank you everyone! I love you all!

Joanne M. Anderson

Prologue

The short book takes place in the fictitious, small town of Bixlerville in rural Pennsylvania. All people characters are fictional, while Noble, Cash, Paloosa and Kazi are true to their equine names, breeds, ages and personalities. It begins in late March and ends on Labor Day.

Some of the Characters

Mandy ~ a 14-year-old 9th grader, is teased relentlessly at school for her height (she was 5' 10 ½" before age 12) by the Wicked Three – her nickname for Jennifer, Amanda and Kerry, the pretty and popular girls. But, when they learn about Noble and the Noble Spirit Horse Club, they want to join and be friends.

Colonel Paul ~ is a 38-year-old man who, in jeans, a gray plaid flannel shirt and worn cowboy boots, tosses a duffle bag and a few books into the front seat of his 1998 Ford Ranger. Along with two boxes of personal effects and one vinyl hangup bag, this constitutes his life belongings. He waves good-bye to the Veteran's Administration hospital which has been his home for the past 10 months and swings southeast on I-76, heading for his first civilian job.

Matthew James and Natalie B. Adams ~ sign their names a dozen times, shake hands with the attorney in the room, and walk out as owners of a 452-acre tract of land with a dilapidated farm on State Highway 24 outside the town of Bixlerville. They have a light lunch and toast a new lifestyle ahead before going their separate ways – she to her own attorney office and he to the airport a couple hours away, where he is scheduled to pilot the next flight to Hong Kong.

Carol Gardner ~ looks at the clock, then at the bottle of wine. 10:55 a.m. It is okay, she convinces herself, to have a small drink this close to lunch. She looks around her beautiful house, sunshine streaming in oversized windows, no expense spared on furnishings. She turns on Bruce Springsteen music to take her mind off the unhappiness as she slowly picks up the corkscrew. She supposes this is not a good idea, and at that moment, she doesn't care.

Kate Dawson ~ works hard sorting, coding and filing medical bills at her in-home business before doing her online lessons. She is determined to create a meaningful life for her and her daughter, Anne, in their new location. She hears a vehicle enter her driveway, then a car door shut, then a knock at the door. She sits motionless at her computer. Another knock. A few minutes later, she hears the car drive away, and she begins to cry.

Big Dan ~ racks his brain every day on his truck driver job for how he can start a business or make more money. Without a college education, he knows options are limited. He has to create his own opportunity. But what? How? He has a family to support, and the work is steady and not difficult. Little does he know that he'll be laid off in two weeks.

Manuel Perez ~ works hard in his Perez Brothers Fencing business. He is living his dream of being an entrepreneur in the USA. He sends some money back to his elderly parents, and much of his extended family has emigrated to work and live with him. Some are here legally. Some are not.

The Real Horses

Noble ~ a majestic, dark brown, 20-year-old Thoroughbred, blind in the right eye. Former show jumper and lesson horse. He came 300 pounds underweight with hooves in poor condition. Within five months, he rounded out to 1,340 pounds at 16 hands. At the two year mark, his front shoes were removed permanently, and he goes barefoot, protected by Cavallo® boots on rocky trails. Not a trail horse by training or breed, Noble's gentle nature, willing mind and long legs carry Joanne or her friends up and down trails, through creeks and rivers, over fallen tree limbs and across pastures.

Cash ~ a solid, stocky, chestnut, work horse-pony cross, 22, was rescued for $60 after being given to the Virginia-Maryland Regional College of Veterinary Medicine in Blacksburg, which had no use for him. He was known to have a choking problem, and he has major spook issues. It took a year to catch him, another year to calm him, two more years of round pen work, and in the fifth year of owning him, Joanne began riding. Still a handful for this novice rider, they prefer the containment of trails over open pastures. He never tires, earning him the nickname, Energizer Bunny-Horse and Power Pony. Measuring just a whisker under 15 hands high, Cash weighs exactly 1,000 pounds. His history is unknown, and it has always been obvious that he's desperate for love and leadership.

Paloosa ~ The Appaloosa horse is known for its spotted coloring, great disposition, endurance and versatility, and Paloosa embraces all those qualities and more. She is most unusual in her bronze and creamy coat with a blond mane, and she is the most willing of horses to try anything. Her owner acquired her at age 5; owner was 12. In the past 8 years, Paloosa has learned to go English and Western, though both much prefer bareback with just a hackamore (no bit) to gallop, jump, wade through water and tackle challenging trails. They run barrels, compete often (garnering more than two dozen ribbons) or simply walk along with other riders anywhere, any time, in almost any weather. She is owned by Summer D. of Blacksburg, Virginia.

Kazi ~ the short version of T.D. Kaszandra, her registered Arabian name. At 20, this beautiful, all white, alpha mare has had three foals, the last one having been carried by a palomino Tennessee Walker. The Virginia-Maryland College of Veterinary Medicine performed the embryo transplant at one week from conception, and the surrogate mother foaled on April 6, 2009. Her current owners acquired Kazi at age 9 ½ with no training. "Besides being beautiful, she is gentle, sweet-natured and intelligent," they report. "Until you've seen her run full out with her tail flagged, head high and nostrils flaring, you have missed one of nature's most spectacular creations!" Kazi has taken

blue ribbons and a trophy in trail competitions and English halter. She stands at 14.2 hands, weighs 925 pounds and has retired from competition due to laminitis issues, the same reason she could not carry her foal. She is owned by Donnie and Diane C. of Dublin, Va.

A Noble Spirit

Chapter

1

She walked slowly into the house, dropped her backpack by the kitchen table and climbed the stairs to her bedroom, her shoulders slumped. Her mother watched from behind the sewing machine. Her older brother Danny appeared a couple minutes later, slid off his backpack with a "Hi, Mom," before grabbing a glass and reaching for the refrigerator.

"Kids making fun of Mandy again?" Martha asked, already knowing the answer by her daughter's glum return from the school day.

"Yeah, those same three girls mostly. Usually they snicker behind her back, but today after lunch and after school they approached and asked about the view way up there and called her a bean pole," he responded, referring to Mandy's five-foot, 10 ½ -inch height. At 14, she'd been that tall more than two years, way higher than anyone in her ninth grade class and maybe the whole school, except for Mrs. Engels, the music teacher, and Mr. Johnson, the science teacher. Oh, and the part-time basketball coach. She even towered over the principal.

"Jennifer seems to be the ring leader. Ya know, Mom, I don't get it," he said, plopping his own 6-foot frame backwards on a kitchen chair. "She is the most beautiful girl in the whole school, maybe in the whole state, and she can sing as well as Taylor Swift. But she looks angry if she looks at you. She looks sad if you catch her looking away, out the window or something. She's gorgeous and talented, but she doesn't even look pretty to me because she's not very nice. Does that make sense?"

"Yes, it does, Danny," his mother replied, "because our real character, the essence of who we are, radiates from within. It doesn't matter how we look on the outside, and sadly, some of the prettiest people in the world on the outside are not really the most beautiful people at all."

Mandy changed out of her navy blue skirt, lime green tee and print blouse, hung them neatly and slipped into faded jeans, an old brown tee shirt and gray hoodie sweatshirt. She let a few more tears flow before wiping her face, blowing her nose and walking downstairs.

"Hey, sweet pea," said her mom softly, "come look at this." She directed Mandy to her sewing corner, intending to distract her from the negative talk of the school girls. "I got the ribbon on the bodice today." She picked up the top of what would be a bridal gown of organza and lace, accented with ribbon embedded horizontally to create an empire style waist. The same ribbon would flow vertically down the skirt. The bride intended to wear matching ribbons in her hair and around her bouquet.

"Oh, it's beautiful, Mom," said Mandy, admiring her mother's work. "I hope some day I can have just as beautiful a wedding dress with ribbons and lace just like this one!"

"That's what you said about the last one, that satin gown with a row of pearls down the single shoulder strap and across the sweetheart neckline," Martha replied.

"They are all so pretty. I wonder what it is like to be dressed up in such amazing gowns," Mandy continued, picking up a piece of fabric, holding it in front of her and twirling around the room. Martha delighted in seeing her smile and dance and forget for a moment the ugliness of some insensitive kids. "Do you want some milk or juice and a cookie?"

"Can I take it with me, please?" Mandy asked, as she pulled

down a jar, lid and small, plastic baggie. Her mom nodded, and the tall girl tightened the lid on some juice, put two cookies in the baggie and picked up an apple, placing it all in a old green backpack that hung by the back door next to a parka, an old raincoat and some ballcaps. "I'll be back by supper," she waved as she gaily hopped down the back steps and headed up the big hill behind the house.

Mandy was lucky, she thought on the way up, the school incident already forgotten in her excitement. Unlike most of her friends, she didn't have to do her homework when she got home from school. Her parents felt that she needed a break between school and more school - homework - so she was allowed to ride her bike, play ball with the dog, read one of her horse books, hang out with friends, bake cookies, play games with Danny – almost anything except television or computer games. They weren't forbidden, just discouraged as not especially valuable or worthwhile.

Her current, favorite, after-school activity was walking about a half-mile to the top of the big hill behind her house. She would zigzag because it was so steep in places, then walk through a little wooded section to look down on the renovation taking place at a once-abandoned farm.

She pulled out a faded, aqua beach towel and plastic garbage bag to put on the ground first. She laid them neatly on an already-matted section about three feet from a broken fence. The bag kept the towel from getting damp on the spring ground. She would lie here on her stomach most afternoons, propped on her elbows, watching below while she munched on her snack. Sometimes she'd read -- or re-read -- one of her horse books. She could only imagine riding a horse, wind in its mane and her hair, a feeling of freedom, moving at lightning speed on a majestic animal of which there was no match on earth, Mandy was certain.

There was a farmhouse of substantial size with paint peeling, a couple screen windows dangling and a bunch of overgrown shrubs obscuring the one side of the house she could see. She also could see the front door and a sweeping front porch with columns and what looked like lace, wood inserts in the corners. She could tell it had been a very pretty house at one time. A small, log cabin was situated on the other side of an overgrown pasture. The best looking building was the barn because, typical of Pennsylvania style, it had a solid stone foundation that went half way up the sides. Four other buildings of various sizes and states of disrepair, along with woods and fields completed the picture.

Her father said he heard the people who bought the property were going to make a horse farm out of it. Mandy didn't know what kind of a horse farm, but she couldn't wait to climb up here every day, watching patiently for a horse. In the past three weeks, old broken cars, a rusty school bus and other junk had been hauled away. Fences were repaired and replaced, and when they were hammering and moving near her favorite spot, she grabbed her stuff and stashed it in the woods. Then she climbed an old apple tree and watched from up there, no one aware that a young, very tall, horse crazy girl was enthralled with all the buzz at the old farm. Well, not quite no one.

The man who appeared to be directing the fence repair – telling the other three guys which boards to remove and replace and which ones to tighten up – spoke in English and Spanish and walked with a limp. She saw him pause and look intently at the matted grass spot near the edge of the fence. His eyes swept from side to side suspiciously. She wiggled her way around the not-very-wide tree trunk to hide as much as she could.

She was pretty sure no one saw her. The lead man, however, estimated her age, height and weight from seeing just part of a sneaker, a hand clinging to a tree branch on the side and a snippet of wavy brown, shoulder length hair. He figured she was young and tall and laid on the trampled grass often.

When she ventured a look again, they had finished near her and were moving along toward the corner, where in some sections, there was no fence at all that she could see. A banged up pick-up truck moved along slowly in front of them with new posts, boards and tools in the back. The door had "Perez Brothers Fencing" painted in white letters. The man with the limp took note of her out of the corner of his eye as she climbed down out of the tree.

Over the next several weeks, crews of men arrived in trucks daily and tossed appliances and junk out of the house, cabin and barn and hauled it away. They tore down one of the outbuildings, then braced a couple more, put new roofs on the house and the big barn, and mowed, then dug up the pasture between the house and the cabin. Mandy was in school the day they replaced the fencing around this pasture and poured on what looked like a foot or more of some sort of gray sand. She was there the afternoon a roller drove all over it, pressing it down, and then it struck her! An arena! A horse arena!

She was practically breathless when she arrived home for supper. "There's an arena, Mom, Dad, Danny, it really is going to be a horse farm!! Can I quit school and get a job there?" she asked. Everyone laughed, and after her dad said grace, they dove into Martha's homemade chicken pot pie and a salad followed by ice cream they made last Sunday. They always did something as a family Sundays after church and lunch, and last week, it was making peach ice cream with the pastor's family.

"Do you know the girl who moved into that bright, blue house over on Newport Street a couple months ago?" her father asked Mandy.

Mandy could see that street and the wickedly wild blue colored house down the other side from the top of the big hill before she went through the woods to overlook the farm. "Well, I know her name is Anne Dawson, and I think she lives there with her mother. She's a grade behind me. Why?"

"Someone at the shop mentioned having groceries delivered to that house once every two weeks. No one ever sees anyone go in or out, except for the girl taking the bus to school," her dad explained.

The shop he was talking about was a machine shop that made custom parts for a variety of farm and manufacturing equipment. Her father had been their mechanic and truck driver for seven years, picking up and delivering parts and finished products all over the region and neighboring counties, as well as maintaining the three delivery trucks.

Mandy and Danny walked to school a few blocks away, but for Anne it would be a mile or more. The number eight school bus circled through the east part of the town and returned on Newport Street. The bright blue house was the last stop each morning and afternoon.

"Anne keeps to herself," Danny piped up. "She's real cute, but very shy and goes right from the bus to homeroom. I think she's the first one on the bus every afternoon. I see her walking with Emily Porter. They're both in 8th grade."

Emily was the pastor's daughter, and she was always nice to everyone. She spoke sweetly to Mandy, too, and never mentioned her height, though there was more than a foot and a half difference.

The Porters had been in town for six years. Her father replaced the retiring minister at Amethyst Valley Bible Church. Mr. Porter was working as a sports writer in Boston when he felt called to the ministry. After uprooting his young family from their New England home to attend Dallas Theological Seminary, he accepted the pastor position at this small-town Pennsylvania church. Since his arrival, the congregation had grown steadily; such was the draw of his basic Bible teaching.

Mandy had always gone to the little church, and she loved the Porters. Emily was the oldest of five children, one of those families where all the kids look alike. You could pick out a Porter child by the freckles, sandy-coppery hair and blue sparkly eyes. And there were two more on the way, twins due in about two months. Mandy once wondered how they managed to feed them all, since her family only had two kids and with her father's truck driving job and her mother's in-home sewing business, they never seemed to have much extra money.

Mandy had everything she needed, however, including pretty dresses and shirts that her mother made. She loved that she didn't have to shop at the mall stores for two reasons. One was that she never had anything that looked like anyone else's clothes. And the second was her height. Her mother made blouses and skirts, pants, dresses and jumpers tailored to her size and frame. All the store dresses for her age were way too short or simply didn't fit comfortably.

The only thing that Mandy longed for was a horse. She lived and dreamed about horses since riding one – not even a real one - for 25 cents outside a discount store when she was 3. Every birthday, she only wanted a model horse or a horse book. Her mother made curtains, pillowcases and toss pillows for her room in horse fabric.

When she went to the county fair each summer, she used all her tickets for carousel rides and twice rode a live pony in a small pen.

Her imagination would carry her through mountains, along beaches, across grassy pastures and into wooded trails on horseback. Other times, she just imagined walking down a dirt road leading her horse, or reading a book while the horse grazed nearby. She saw a picture once of a girl reading a book while lying on her horse's back. Now there was some reality to her horse dreams. A horse farm over the big ridge from her house!

Martha had been so committed in recent months with alterations and bridal gowns that she realized she had neglected to call on the new tenants in that blue house. She drove by there often on her way to and from the fabric store. She never saw anyone, but she didn't especially look either. The previous renters had a couple rough kids, and no one was displeased that they moved away after painting it that wild, brilliant blue.

"I'll call Mrs. Porter to see if she knows the lady and take some muffins or something over soon," she stated, determined not to let her sewing business crowd out her civic and Christian duty of being a good neighbor. And she was a bit curious about Anne and the mother whom no one saw.

Martha's Chicken Pot Pie

Mix together in a large bowl:
3 cups chopped cooked chicken
2 10.75-oz. cans cream of chicken soup
1 10.5-oz. can condensed chicken broth
1 15-oz. can mixed vegetables, frozen
½ tsp. poultry seasoning
Spread chicken mixture in greased 13x9 glass pan

Blend in large bowl:
2 cups biscuit mix
8 oz. sour cream
1 cup milk
Spoon this mix in dollops on top of chicken and swirl
with back of spoon to cover entirely

Bake at 350° for 50-60 minutes.

Chapter 2

Over the next two weeks, the farmhouse was scraped and painted white with black shutters and a red front door. The windows were replaced, and the front porch restored to a wonderful, shaded place for rockers and flower pots – which arrived the day after Mandy thought it looked like a wonderful place to read a horse book. Five white rockers with navy and aqua cushions were complemented with big flower pots, which later in the spring were stuffed with red and white geraniums and blue lobelia falling out over the rims. A flag pole and American flag were mounted on the column at the corner, giving the house a very patriotic appeal.

She saw what seemed like hundreds of bales of hay unloaded at the upper level of the barn, and she just knew she would see a horse soon. Except for those two pony rides at the county fair when she was little and watching horses from a horse club 20 miles away ride in her town's annual 4th of July parade, Mandy had not really been near a horse.

It was a sunny Thursday afternoon when Mandy saw two horse trailers parked near the barn. She then spotted four horses grazing next to the arena, which had been outfitted with a three-step block and some barrels and poles for jumps. One new bench and four black, wrought iron chairs were sitting in a row just outside the fence. Two horses grazed together – a white one and a creamy, bronze speckled one. Mandy thought from her horse books that the white one was an Arabian. Maybe the other one was an Appaloosa, but she hadn't seen that color before. Most of the pictures showed gray and white Appaloosas. "Tomorrow, I'll ask to borrow Dad's binoculars," she thought, "and bring a book on horse breeds."

A little farther away from them was a palomino and beyond that a large, beautiful brown horse with a blond mane and tail. He might be a Rocky Mountain, she figured, and the palomino could be lots of different breeds. They ate grass, and Mandy dreamed.

Her daydream turned to a sleepy dream, as she drifted off on her old beach towel near the fence overlooking what was now Amethyst Valley Horse Farm. She awoke with a start. Leaves were rustling nearby. She heard a crunching sound. She backed down her towel a few inches and looked around. She wasn't dreaming now.

To her left about 12 feet away, she saw a front hoof step into view, then another one. She backed into a crouch and followed the legs up to a muscular chest, a long neck and the most beautiful horse head she had ever seen. He was alert, ears perked forward, listening, sensing someone or something nearby.

Mandy quietly and slowly stood up as the horse moved forward into full view. That's when she noticed his light-blue, white eye that wasn't an eye at all. Her heart was pounding as she stood just two feet away. The large horse raised his head over the top fence rail and turned far enough around that she could see a perfect, brown eye and the thin, white blaze meandering up its face, ending just above his eyes. He was looking at her, and she was looking at him. She put her hand out slowly, then remembering that she had her apple core, she reached in the backpack.

"Hi, I'm Mandy, and you can have my apple core," she said softly, stepping tentatively forward and extending her hand. He stretched his neck over the top rail in her direction. She moved closer until his lips gently removed the apple core. His muzzle was soft, very gentle and barely whisked her palm to retrieve the apple piece. She didn't want to wash that hand ever again.

He contentedly chewed on it and reached for another one. "I don't have any more," Mandy explained, "but I can bring some tomorrow." He seemed to understand. Without moving his feet, he lowered his head on his side of the fence and started eating grass. Mandy spoke to him through the fence and ventured closer. Thinking he could not see her, she spoke louder before placing her hand on the top of his leg. His skin quivered just a little, but he didn't move away. She kept talking, then started singing the first quiet song that came to mind - "Amazing Grace" - and softly petted his leg and side.

When she stood up - all her five feet 10 ½ inches - her face was just at the side of his neck. For the first time in her life, she was okay with being tall. He seemed tall. He was taller than the fair ponies or carousel horses. From that day forward, she did not care what Jennifer, Amanda or Kerry – the Wicked Three in her mind – had to say about her or her height. She simply lived to see and pet this horse she called Gentle Giant.

Every day after school for three weeks and on Saturdays, Mandy went up the big hill, and every day Gentle Giant came to the fence for some apple or carrot. This day, while he grazed next to the fence, Mandy climbed the fence post. She had wondered all along if he'd ever been ridden or what happened to his eye and how come he was not with the other horses. She had read about horses being herd animals, and how being solitary was not good for them. They needed socialization on some level, and they felt safer with other horses.

He always seemed so calm and sweet, and she felt a real kinship with him. She knew what it was like to be different, to be singled out from the rest. Mandy looked up horse disabilities on the Internet and read that sometimes horses are excluded from a herd because they are different, unequal, weaker in some way. She loved him like she'd never loved any animal or thing in her whole life.

She stroked his withers and mane from her perch on the top fence rail. Then, almost without thinking, she jumped down on his side of the fence. It startled Gentle Giant, and he skittered a few feet away. Mandy walked around him so he could see her. With the last piece of apple from her pocket, she coaxed him back next to the fence, but with his sighted eye next to the rail. She climbed back up on the fence, grabbed tightly on to his mane, and slid her right leg over his huge, high back. He stood still.

Mandy pulled herself over on him and held on tightly, scarcely daring to breathe, grateful for her long legs ever so gently draped down the sides of his belly. Then she remembered in her reading that instructors are always telling new riders "don't forget to breathe." She would wonder how anyone could "forget to breathe," and here she was, sitting on Gentle Giant, looking at the ground that seemed to be half a mile below her, holding her breath.

"Hey, you, what are you doing? Who do you think you are? You're trespassing, and you're on a horse that doesn't belong to you. Get off and get going!" She heard a gruff voice from behind her and in turning to look, she loosened her grip and fell to the ground.

Chapter

3

Mandy got up and brushed herself off and stood up, tall. She looked directly into the eyes of the man she'd seen directing the fence repair and walking in and out of the cabin many times. She figured he lived there, and maybe he was the farm manager, since he didn't often go into the big house. She'd also seen him working with the other horses in the arena and in a smaller, round, fenced area. He motioned for them to run circles around him, and when he stopped, the horse would walk to him. When he turned his back and walked away, the horse followed. She was amazed, looking through her dad's binoculars. She couldn't ever hear him, but he seemed to have a mild manner and kind way with the horses, nothing like how he just sounded.

Now, they faced off next to Gentle Giant grazing peacefully, unaware, it seemed, that they were there or even that she'd fallen off his right side.

"My-my-my name is Mandy, uh, Mandy Sullivan," she stammered. "I live at the bottom of that big hill," she continued, waving her arm behind her. "I've read about and dreamed of horses all my life (hoping that 'all her life' sounded older than 14 years. For the third time in recent days, she was glad to be tall, knowing that she looked older than she really was). "I've been coming up here every day watching the farm being fixed up. And when I met Gentle Giant, well, I fell in love, and I see him every day, and I'm sorry I trespassed, and I apologize for upsetting you."

The man's face softened, and he took a step forward. "Sorry I spoke so roughly, young lady, but horses can be dangerous animals, and you can't just hop on one you don't know. How many times have you done that?" he asked.

"Just today. Today was the first time. Honest. I had to turn him around, because I don't think he can see on his right side," she said, half asking.

"You are right, um, Mandy. This horse isn't good any more for show jumping, so he's up for sale, and some folks are coming today to look at him. I need to take him now." He walked past her, put a halter on the horse and began leading him away, limping slightly every time his left foot stepped down, just as she'd noticed the day the fences were fixed.

"Wait, wait, please wait," she cried. Gathering herself together, she asked in her most adult voice, "How much are you asking for Gentle Giant?"

"His name is Noble, and the price is $2,000," the man stated.

"Two thousand dollars for a horse that's half blind?" she said incredulously. She never heard of so much money.

"Noble has lots and lots of fine training," the man explained, "and he's a very calm Thoroughbred. He will be perfect for a beginner or intermediate rider who doesn't mind a very tall horse and isn't interested in riding in the show circuit." He turned and continued limping away, Noble obediently following, his soft, dark brown tail swaying with each step.

Mandy went through the fence and threw herself sobbing on the old beach towel. She didn't care that a light rain had dampened it, and she was getting wet and dirty. Her sweatshirt and jeans were already grass stained from falling off Gentle Giant, uh, er, Noble. She never cried so much or so hard when the kids made fun of her height as she cried now. She knew Noble wasn't hers, and it had only been a few weeks, but she needed him. He took away all her insecurities and uncertainty about being tall, about not being the brightest and best in her class. She didn't bother trying out for the cheerleading team, and she knew her parents couldn't afford braces for her slightly, uneven teeth. None of that mattered when she was on her hilltop hideout with Noble.

She knew it wasn't God's will that she pray for stuff, like a horse or a new bike, so she decided to pray for Noble. She folded her hands and bowed her head.

"Dear God," she began. "This is Mandy. I'm 14, and I love horses. I guess you know this because Daddy says you know everything, and we can talk to you about anything. I'm praying today for my gentle giant, Noble. Is it okay to pray for an animal? I hope so. I am praying that he can stay here and that somehow he can be mine. He is missing one of his eyes, you see, well, I guess you already know that, and I'm too tall for my age, and you probably know that, too, and we just bonded, and we belong together, and can you please fix this? The pastures here are good now, and it is the best place for him to live, I think. So I am praying that you will let him live here and that these people do not want to buy him. I love you, God. Even though I'm tall, I feel very, very small right now. Love, Mandy. Amen."

She gathered up her wet towel, cramming it into the backpack and started through the woods into a steady rain and down the hill. Tears were still stinging her eyes, and she was not paying attention. The grass was wet in the steep section, and she slipped, rolling and tumbling without control until she hit a rock and stopped with a thud on her left side. The backpack went flying, and pain shot up her left arm.

"Mandy is not back from her hilltop climb to watch the activity at the new horse farm," Martha said to Danny when she finished setting the table and turned the hamburgers. "Supper will be ready in five minutes. Will you please call her or walk up there and find her? She seems to have lost all reason over this horse obsession, and now it's pouring."

"Sure, Mom," said Danny, grabbing the old raincoat and striding out the back door, calling to Mandy on his way up the path. "Ma-a-a-andy, Ma-a-a-andy, suppertime, sis," he yelled.

Mandy sat up and screamed, "Danny, Danny, up here. I'm hurt."

Danny broke into a run, uphill, in the rain, his 16-year-old legs sprinting underneath him. He reached her in two minutes flat. It seemed like an hour to Mandy, who was holding her left arm tightly to her chest and crying.

"What have you done? Are you okay?" Danny shouted above the noise of the downpour.

"I wasn't paying attention, and I fell, and they might sell Gentle Giant, and the man took him away to the farm, and my arm hurts terribly bad, and I don't know what to do," she wailed.

"Settle down, little sis, calm down." He picked up the wet, muddy backpack, which was a good 10 feet below her and reached for her.

"Hand me your good arm, and let me lift you to your feet," he instructed his crying sister, both of them soaked to the skin now. He held her right arm and around her waist and supported her as best he could as they carefully and slowly made their way down the hill.

Martha was at the back door. "I heard you yell, sweet pea, are you okay?"

"I think she broke her arm," Danny said. "She slipped, and it looks like she tumbled a bit and busted her arm on a rock that stopped her."

Her face had a few scratches, and she screamed when Martha tried to look at or move her arm. Her father watched everything from the kitchen doorway before walking over, putting his arm around his soaking wet daughter and telling Danny to go open his truck door. He would take Mandy to the hospital. Martha grabbed some clean, dry clothes from her room and tucked a blanket around her. Once she was settled in the truck safely, she and Danny retreated to the house for a couple of over-cooked burgers.

Her dad wasn't sure if his precious daughter was crying more about the pain in her arm or the pain that seemed to be consuming her heart over this horse she met just a few weeks ago. He was a little ashamed as the thought crossed his mind of what this medical expense would mean. He had been laid off from his truck driving job at the shop earlier in the day. Mr. Morton was real sorry. He said it was a terribly difficult decision, but with a slow economy and all, they had to cut out something, so they were asking customers to pick up and deliver their own parts. Mandy's dad's job had been eliminated, and they planned to sell the three trucks.

The ER doctor was a strikingly handsome man, about six feet tall with a full head of unruly, blond hair, bright, gray-green eyes and a name tag: Samuel Gardner, M.D. He examined Mandy's arm carefully, listening to her story of running down the hill, crying about a horse, not paying attention, while her father sat nearby filling out forms and signing for treatment. "The x-rays will show the precise angle and severity of the break. My best guess is that it's the radius. Kids heal well at this age – at least those who follow doctor's orders," he said, smiling.

Following two hours of ER activity and a few x-rays, an orthopedic surgeon showed up to set Mandy's broken radius. She and her father returned home close to midnight, her new, light blue cast wrapping around the base of her thumb and ending just below the elbow. She fell asleep only after another prayer for Noble not to be sold.

Her arm throbbed so much in the morning that Martha decided Mandy should stay home from school. It was Friday anyway, and she asked Danny to get homework assignments from Mandy's teachers if he could. Her father had already left the house at his regular work time, though he wasn't going to work any more. He would be paying a visit to Pastor Porter and a couple buddies who might know who needed a reliable, experienced mechanic or driver.

"I want to go up the hill, Mom, and see if Noble is still there," Mandy said, her eyes pleading for permission.

"I am taking some of the carrot walnut muffins to Mrs. Dawson this morning, Mandy. You rest. After lunch, I will walk with you to the top of the hill. You must prepare yourself that the gentle giant horse may have moved away," she responded.

"I know, but I have to know," Mandy mumbled as she crawled on the couch and pulled a green and yellow patchwork quilt over her. Her mom tucked her in and spoke more sternly than she normally did, reminding Mandy she was not to leave the house until Martha returned.

"I promise, Mom," Mandy said quietly, snuggling down and letting her mother place a pillow under the broken arm.

Martha had called Mrs. Porter, the pastor's wife, and asked if she had met Mrs. Dawson, and she had not.

"I went over a couple weeks ago, when I heard the same as you, Martha," Beverly Porter had told her. "No one answered the door, but I had the feeling that someone was home. I didn't dare leave a plate of cookies outside, so I brought them back and left a note in the door that I'd come to extend a welcome and invite her to church."

Martha put the muffins in a cake pan, covered it with plastic wrap and drove to the bright blue house on Newport Street. There was a green Mercury Sable parked at the back of the driveway, and the front of the house was neat and tidy. As she approached the front door, it opened, and a pretty woman not more than 30 years old stood there.

"Hello, I'm Martha Sullivan. I've brought some muffins and want to tell you welcome to town. I believe your daughter is at the same school as my son and daughter," she said.

"You're very kind. I'm Kate Dawson. Please come in," and with that, she opened the front door and took the cake pan with the muffins. Martha stepped into an immaculate living room, simply and comfortably furnished in soft rust, navy blue and cream, a welcome relief from the brash blue exterior. Following Kate through to a large kitchen, Martha noticed a small home office and what appeared to be a girl's bedroom with horse posters on one wall.

The kitchen was equally as neat and tidy, and Kate took two cups and saucers from a cupboard. "Would you like a cup of coffee or tea?" she asked. Not seeing a coffeemaker on the counter and taking note of the large, glass canister of tea bags, Martha said tea would be fine. Kate pulled down a white teapot, lined a basket with a cloth napkin and put four muffins in it, retrieving a butter dish from the cupboard.

She went on to set a small, green tray with honey, cream, spoons, knives and calico print, cloth napkins and two small plates. She walked to a little, enclosed porch off the kitchen, and Martha carried the basket and butter. There was just room for a bistro table and two chairs, a plant stand with a Boston fern, one wicker cushioned chair and side table with a *National Geographic* magazine and a Dick Francis novel.

Kate returned to the kitchen for the teapot and cups and saucers. They exchanged information about their kids and discovered both daughters were crazy about horses. Martha told her about the new horse farm, the gentle giant horse named Noble and Mandy's broken arm.

They chatted like a couple old friends, until Kate rather abruptly turned away and stopped talking. She slowly looked at Martha, eyes brimming with tears.

A Noble Spirit

Chapter
4

Martha just naturally extended her hand to the attractive, young woman's arm, whose story spilled out. She married her high school sweetheart after graduation. Anne was born the next year when Kate was just 19. Two years later, she began having panic attacks and anxiety about leaving home.

"I thought I was going crazy," she tearfully continued. "My husband didn't understand it. I didn't understand it. We'd go out, and I got sweaty and my heart beat fast, and I thought I was going to die. I'd run out of a movie theatre or restaurant and scream to be taken home. I tried therapy, and we went to counseling. We divorced five years later."

Martha sipped her tea and waited. Kate continued. "Kevin drifted away, and when he married a young woman with two kids in the same town, and Anne got into trouble at school, I decided to move – in part to force myself out of my rut. I've read all I could find about panic attacks and agoraphobia, but it's still with me. I planned to move near my sister, Donna, outside Pittsburgh. I've always been nice and as generous as I could be with them and their 7-year-old twins whom Anne adores. Her husband, Brad, however, discouraged me from any move in their direction. They have lots of money, too, and, well, ..." she trailed off.

Kate swallowed hard, sat up straight and smiled. "You know, you get to pick your friends and your pets, but not your family. My mom and I went to garage sales and thrift stores before the move, and one of my brothers drove over with us in a rented truck. We are both excited to be out of apartment life, though what about this wild blue house color?" They both chuckled. "I think that's why the rent is reasonable. Anyway, it's my new beginning, but I'm sort of stuck in the starting gate. I'm determined to get over this, Martha, or at least learn to cope. It's hard. I feel isolated - and inferior."

Martha patted her arm and reassured her that she now had her first real friend in Bixlerville. She had an aunt with agoraphobia who didn't travel alone and seemed to experience anxiety in common situations. Martha saw firsthand her mother and grandmother's annoyance with the situation. She sympathized with the limitations – real or imagined – that her aunt endured, while no one in the family made any effort to learn about or understand it.

Kate apologized. "I am sorry to have dumped this on you. I don't know my way around yet, so I don't go out. I only feel safe at home, and my main concern is for Anne. She's just 13, and she needs her own friends and school activities."

"Well, I planned to invite you to the ladies Bible study group that meets every other Wednesday evening," Martha stated. "Perhaps you would ride with me. It's just a couple miles from here at Beverly Porter's house. She's the pastor's wife, and she came by with cookies recently."

Kate remembered. "I was feeling nervous that day. I wanted to answer the door, but I did not. I work from home doing medical billing, and it was an especially busy week. I also take classes online with Penn Foster College toward a veterinary technician associate degree."

Martha told Kate about Mandy walking up the big hill every afternoon to watch the new horse farm activities and visit the gentle giant horse, which might have been sold yesterday. "We live at the bottom of the other side of the same hill behind your house. We are going to walk up this afternoon to see if the horse is still there. Why don't we meet up there at 3:30 when Anne will be home from school? Then, we'll go through the woods and look for the horse and see the horse farm together."

Kate smiled before frowning. "I will try, but that's a big hill, and it's a long ways up there, and I'm not sure I can do it. I will try," she repeated, forcing a small smile.

At 3:15 that afternoon, Mandy put on her sling to stabilize the arm, packed her backpack, and she and Martha started up the hill. Fifteen minutes later, they were standing at the top, looking down at the bright blue house. There was no one outside. No sign of movement.

"C'mon, Mom, we are so close. Just through the woods. I have to go see," Mandy was nearly frantic.

"Mandy," said Martha. "We will wait here for 10 minutes. It is important that we be dependable friends for Kate and Anne. Please sit down."

Mandy pulled out the old beach towel for them to sit on. "I don't know what's so scary about walking up a hill," she said. "It's practically part of her back yard."

"It's not about the hill, sweet pea, it's about moving away from a place where you feel very safe," Martha tried to explain. "It's about pushing yourself outside of your comfort zone. You have not experienced anything like this, and I've only read about it, but we need to help if we can." They waited all 10 minutes before standing up.

Mandy picked up the towel, and they started to walk away when they heard a faint "hey, hey, up there." Anne was walking away from the back door, and Kate seemed frozen on the back step. Anne stopped. Kate walked down the three steps and stopped. Anne started up the hill. Kate walked toward Anne. In a halting manner of stopping, starting and looking back at her rented blue house – her safe place - get farther from her, Kate continued. Halfway up, she stood still. Anne walked back down to her, took her hand and walked side by side with her. About 20 feet from the top, Kate stopped, a look of terror crossing her face and a large, black snake crossing her path.

A Noble Spirit

Chapter

5

"I want to go home! I'm so scared!" Kate shrieked. Mandy grabbed a stick and ran down, flailing at the snake, which was probably as scared as Kate. Martha was right behind her and gathered Kate in her arms as she wilted in tears and embarrassment.

Mandy turned to Anne. "Those snakes are harmless. They're called blue racers because they have a blue stripe on their bellies. My brother Danny messes around with them all the time. It's okay now."

"Danny is your brother? Danny Sullivan," Anne asked wide-eyed and curious. "The guy with the spiky blond hair who plays baseball?"

"Yep, that's him. But the most important thing today, right now, is to see if my gentle giant horse Noble is still at the farm. Of course, he's not really mine, but I love him more than anything in the world. Mo-o-o-o-om? Can we go now ple-e-e-e-ease???" Mandy pleaded.

Kate had pulled herself together, hugged Martha, and the two were walking the last few feet to the top. "Yes, go ahead," she said.

With that, Mandy started running with Anne at her heels. By the time, the moms got through the woods to the fence, Mandy and Anne were on the other side of it feeding apple pieces to the largest horse Martha had ever seen. It was instantly evident why Mandy called him a gentle giant, though by now they all knew his name was Noble.

"He looks like a Thoroughbred with those long legs, fine, arched neck and muscular build," Kate observed, stepping closer. "Something is wrong with this eye." Mandy turned him around with an apple bribe. "He's blind on the right, but he can see you fine now. He is a Thoroughbred. How did you know?"

"I grew up down the road from a dairy farm that had some horses, and I spent lots of time there. I went to a horse camp for two summers, and I suppose that I'm still a little horse crazy. The Thoroughbreds are tall, like Noble, bred for racing, but they make great jumpers and event horses. Some – the calm ones – are even good trail horses, though they are not as sure-footed as the Arabians or Quarter Horses. When you watch a group of horses run, each one looks beautiful, but you can always pick out a Thoroughbred. They don't simply run; they carry themselves with an elegance of nobility. Some are nervous and high strung, but I can see that Noble is special by his calm attitude. He doesn't even see Anne, and he's perfectly content with her petting him on the other side. Anne, move slowly and walk around the front of him, please. We really don't know anything about Noble at this point."

Martha turned to Mandy. "How do you know he's a Thoroughbred, sweet pea?"

Mandy didn't dare mention that she had climbed on his back once or that she got yelled at by the limping man and fell off, just before her tumble down the hill on her way home. He told her Noble was a Thoroughbred.

Mandy answered slowly and truthfully, "Well, they are tall, like Mrs. Dawson says, and I brought up my horse book a couple times and looked at breeds in photos and compared them to all the horses so I could tell what each one is," all of which was true.

Noble wandered off soon after the apple ran out, and Mandy pulled out her beach towel and laid it horizontally so at least they could all get their elbows on it. She told them all about the restoration of the past weeks. Kate talked about her horse experiences, and Anne said she'd like to be an actress in horse movies.

There they were, two mothers and two daughters, side by side, a bit squished on one beach towel, talking and giggling about horses and farms and hopes and dreams. And the one with a refreshing spirit of hope that day was Kate.

Kate told Martha on the way back that she wasn't ready to go to the Bible study a couple miles away, not just because she might be nervous, but she did not want to leave Anne home alone for an evening. When the group of six ladies convened at Beverly Porter's the following Wednesday, Martha told them how much Kate needed friends, the kind of women who would encourage her and surround her with genuine, non-judgmental friendship. Martha had mentioned how immaculate Kate's house was, and someone suggested they meet there every other week.

Kate was elated with the idea of hostessing an evening group of ladies, but she was equally as hesitant. "I don't know much about the Bible," she confided in Martha. "I haven't been to church in a long time. I'd like Anne to go to Sunday school and church, and me too, but I haven't been able to get out to that yet. I don't think I can contribute much to a study group."

"No worries," Martha reassured her. "Beverly leads it and we have a study book, and besides, you don't study something you already know. We're all learning all the time." And so it was settled. Kate was comfortable in her own home, and she loved entertaining on a small scale. Once again, she was filled with simple joy she hadn't felt in a long time.

She wanted to call her sister and tell her about her new friends and that she walked up this big hill, but they didn't part on good terms when she last left her house, so she repressed the urge. And Donna wouldn't understand about her accomplishment up the hill. For agoraphobic people, going even half a block from home can be frightening. But for non-agoraphobic people, it can all seem controlling and superior, when, in fact, it was all inferior. Agoraphobic people do not feel good about themselves very much.

The new horse farm's general manager, the man with the

limp, had unloaded the boxes from his truck and put them in the cabin. Then he made a couple trips to the discount store for dishes, pots and pans, kitchen utensils, bed linens and curtains and curtain rods. He also bought a couch and chair, a large rug and some smaller ones, a bookcase, table and television set. A thick wood table with three chairs was already in the kitchen of the cabin, and the one woodstove would be sufficient for now. There was a decent bed and dresser in the one bedroom and one wood rocking chair. The horse farm owner promised to have a heat pump and ductwork installed before winter for central heat and air, as well as run cable for the TV and set up wireless Internet. "We'll modernize it," she'd said.

He arranged his books and a few photos on the shelves, and hung two framed prints of horses and one cross stitch. After neatly putting everything away and even hanging curtains, the man looked around, quite pleased with himself. It was cozy. His first home. Small, but how much space does one person need?

Certainly, it was a vast improvement on Army barracks at Fort Bragg, N.C., or a standard issue, dark green cot in a stone fort in a remote province of Afghanistan. He was especially pleased to no longer be a resident of sorts at the VA hospital near Pittsburgh.

The best part of life, however, was the horses. How he had missed them this past year. He was on a pony about the time he learned to walk. From a young age, he observed horse behavior and herd dynamics. He started training a neighbor's horses for free when he was just 11, calmly mimicking the alpha mare in body language, winning their trust in as little as a couple days, depending on the horse. The deal was if he could calm and train eight horses in six months for basic riding and cattle drives, he could pick one for his own. At the end, he chose Brandy, a stocky, dark brown, 8-year-old mustang with a star on his forehead and one white stocking.

Most of the people in his young life had let him down, but never the horses. It was like they strived to understand and respond positively to him, and he always preferred the company of horses to people. The trust went both ways he discovered when he got lost in the Santiago Mountains in the northern part of Big Bend National Park.

He and Brandy took off one day to try out his first camera. The young man had an uncanny sense of direction that failed him that day. It was a few hours before he realized that he really did not know where they were. He headed south for an hour, but as darkness crept in, he decided to spend the night in the shelter of a cliff that angled into a hillside. At first daylight, he simply saddled up, mounted and urged Brandy on with his legs, not even picking up the reins. It seemed all wrong to him, heading west away from the sunrise, but he just sat there and went along for the ride. Sure enough, in just under two hours, Brandy walked on to the road less than a half-mile from the truck and trailer.

He was a senior in high school that fall, and as he drove back home, he pondered the future. There simply had to be more than scraping by in a border town with heat, dust, drugs and poverty rampant all around him.

A Noble Spirit

Chapter
6

Over the next three weeks, Mandy's arm healed, and she visited Noble every afternoon. The Wicked Three at school wanted to know if she's tripped over one of her own long legs. Mandy wanted so much to tell them she broke it when she slid off a gorgeous Thoroughbred horse galloping through the woods in a flowing gown of organza and lace in pursuit of a butterfly or something, but she didn't. Instead, she would think of Noble, half blind, in a pasture by himself, in the dark at night, in pouring rain sometimes, while the other horses had one another's company in the fields below where they would stand tightly together under a tree for protection from wind and rain. Noble would position himself, tail to the wind, and stand alone with his head down.

Noble did not have any company, but he was always calm and nice, and those thoughts gave Mandy enough courage to simply walk away from the Wicked Three. She called it her "Noble Spirit" and embraced it whenever she needed to be strong inside.

Anne Dawson came up to the hilltop hideout some afternoons. She brought a hairbrush one day, and they took turns brushing Noble on his sides and legs. Anne brushed the bottom half of his tail, since she couldn't reach higher, and Mandy would brush the top of his tail and his mane. They hid the brush in a plastic bag at the bottom of the big tree Mandy had climbed.

One afternoon, they climbed on the fence, and Mandy told Anne about getting on Noble's back and falling off when the limpy man yelled at her.

"Can I try it?" Anne queried. "Let's make sure that man isn't coming, and I'll get on. Just for a couple minutes."

Mandy wasn't sure this was a good idea, but the excitement of it got the better of her judgment, and she positioned Noble next to the fence. Then she climbed up next to Anne.

"Hold his mane really tight," she said, adding that she read it doesn't hurt a horse, and it's the best way to mount rather than pulling on the saddle. When you have a saddle, that is.

Anne put one leg on his back, leaned forward and grabbed his mane with both hands. Mandy pushed her over with her good arm, until she was centered on Noble's back. She sat up a little bit, eyes wide with equal amounts of exhilaration and apprehension. Mandy jumped off the fence and stood in front of Noble, hoping he wouldn't try to walk away. He put his head down, and she rubbed his forehead. He seemed quite content and did not move his feet.

"Don't hold your breath, Anne, breathe," Mandy said.

"How did you know I was holding my breath?" Anne asked. "And so, how do I get off?" They decided she should slide off his right side slowly, because Noble was too close to the fence on the left, and let go of the mane as she started moving faster toward the ground. Mandy would help her with her right arm. Anne sat there for five minutes before leaning forward, moving her left leg to the right side of this huge horse and starting to slide. Mandy reached out for her, but Anne was slipping fast. She fell on Mandy, and they both tumbled to the ground, laughing and rolling, narrowly missing the big horse's back legs. For a few minutes, they just laid there on the soft pasture grass, staring at puffy clouds overhead and making up stories about horses and clouds.

Neither was hurt, and they finally retreated to the beach towel to watch the activities below. Mandy was in the habit now of bringing her father's binoculars, so they could see clearly when there was a rider in the arena or the limpy man was doing some training in a small, round, fenced section. Most of the time, they just watched the other horses, grazing and moving around.

They counted 11 horses on this day, and Mandy knew every one of them. Of the original four, she now thought the bronze spotted one was definitely an Appaloosa. The white one's face looked most like an Arabian. The large brown one with the flaxen mane had to be a Rocky Mountain. They come in lots of colors, but the chocolate shades with blond manes are distinctive. She still couldn't be sure what breed the palomino horse was. Maybe a Quarter Horse, maybe a mix of breeds.

The three brown bays looked like show horses, and she'd seen two of them doing figure eights, moving sideways and jumping in the arena. One had a star and two stockings on the back legs. Another had a thin blaze similar to, but straighter than, Noble's, and one was darker brown with one white sock. There was a buckskin she guessed might be a Quarter Horse and another Thoroughbred or maybe Standardbred or Warmblood. She couldn't be sure of that one, but she noticed he was not very obedient to his owner or trainer or whoever was riding him.

A teenage girl rode him occasionally, but he didn't seem to do anything the rider wanted, and she never rode for long. She often hugged the pony which grazed near the horse when he wasn't being ridden or trained. She did not know what breed the pony was. It didn't look like a Haflinger or Fell pony or Icelandic horse. Maybe a Welsh or combination of a small horse and pony. With Noble, that made 11. She wasn't positive of the breeds, of course, but she and Anne compared each horse to pictures in a couple books over and over again, then looked through the binoculars.

They didn't see the limpy man ride. He spent most of his time on the ground in the round pen with different horses at different times. Of course, it wasn't really warm yet either, and it had rained a lot last week, so it might not be good riding weather or footing. At first, Noble was a little frightened when Mandy walked to the fence one day with an umbrella. She put it down quickly, not caring that her ball cap and jacket got wet. She had on good rubber boots, at least. Rain would not keep her away from seeing the gentle giant every day.

During those same weeks, Mandy's dad dropped in on every garage and trucking company within 40 miles of home. The story was always the same: "Wish we had something. Hoping the economy picks up. Leave your name and number. Yes, we understand, even something temporary. Thanks, buddy, for stopping by. Good luck to you." He picked up a few odd runs -- taking a well-to-do gentleman to the airport in Philadelphia and picking him up two weeks later, delivering boxes for a moving company, small stuff, not enough to support his family.

On one overcast Tuesday, he drove by the crispy, new, red, white and blue sign on State Highway 24, a road he knew like the back of his hand. Amethyst Valley Horse Farm. As he passed the driveway, he noticed a few men working on a fence near the road. Well, no harm done by seeing if they needed another hand. He needed work, and it no longer mattered if it were simple labor. He could fix almost anything and figure out whatever he did not already know. He turned around and drove up the winding, gravel driveway to the now picturesque farm.

Three loose horses grazed on the front lawn, one munching on potted plants at the edge of the porch. He saw the empty arena Mandy described, along with vacant pastures on the right and the other horses in a fenced area behind the arena. There was one dark brown horse near the top of the hill. He thought that could be the gentle giant, though he didn't look very big from this distance.

After walking between the horses to the front steps and getting no response from his knocking and ringing the doorbell, Mandy's father walked toward the barn and cabin. There was one truck with "Perez Brothers Fencing" painted on the door and a gray Ford Ranger. Two horse heads poked out over stall doors when he stepped into the barn, and he said: "Anyone here? Hello!"

He walked down the center aisle, and what he thought was a tarp or jacket on the ground at the far end of the barn was a man, crumpled in a ball, holding his belly and moaning. His face was beaded in sweat and contorted with pain.

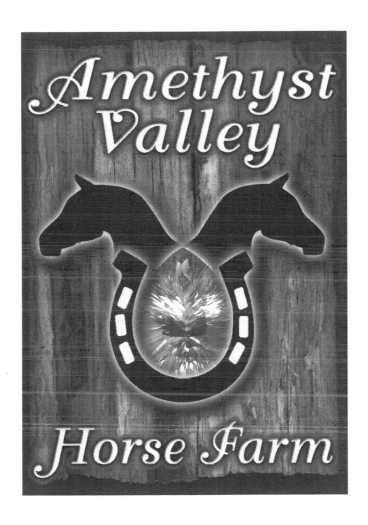

A Noble Spirit

Chapter

7

Mandy's dad leaped forward, dropping to his knees next to the man. "Hey, can you understand me? Should I call 9-1-1? What's the problem?"

"Pain in my belly, terrible pain over here," the man muttered, moving a hand to his right abdomen. "Take me to the hospital? Please?"

They didn't call Mandy's dad Big Dan just to differentiate him from his son Danny. He was a strapping 6-feet 4-inches of strength and stamina. Mandy certainly inherited her height from his side of the family. He bent down to lift the smaller man, surprised that he was so heavy.

"He's got to be solid muscle to the core," Big Dan conjectured, shifting his moaning bundle a couple times, trying not to increase the pain level. He carried the man to his truck and got him situated in the front seat, deciding to forego the seatbelt and let him stay bent over, holding tight to his right side.

"Should I do anything about those horses loose in the front yard?" Big Dan asked.

"Oh, oh. Tell the fence guys to round 'em up somehow when we ride by them on the road," the man responded weakly.

Big Dan swung out of the driveway and pulled to the side of the highway. He jumped out of the truck and yelled at the men, waving and pointing. "We need help putting horses in a pasture, over by the house. This man is very sick."

They looked at him, and one said "no Inglés." The man doubled over in the front seat said to Big Dan: "Repeat this." He spoke slowly, stopping after every couple syllables for Dan to shout the best he could, copying the sounds. "Caballos sueltos. Vete a la casa. Encerra los caballos en la parcela, y cierra la verja. Corre. Date prisa!" The men dropped their tools and ran for the house. Big Dan got in and drove through town as fast as he dared to the hospital.

He pulled up right at the emergency room door and jumped out. A man and a woman strode out, grabbing a gurney from between the outer doors when Big Dan told them he had a badly hurt man in the truck. He stood back and let the hospital staff move the man to the portable bed and wheel him inside. As they moved him, he again noticed the prosthetic device on his lower left leg. He must be the man Mandy described as walking with a limp whom she saw most afternoons. Of course, she had not said she ever met him.

After parking the truck, Big Dan went in to see if he could be of assistance. A nurse handed him the man's wallet and asked him to find out who he was and where he lived.

"Oh, I'm not comfortable with going through a man's private things, ma'am," he said kindly.

"Well, you better get comfortable right now. He's in a lot of pain. We need to determine what's wrong, what course of action to take, whom to call, and we need to know who he is and if he's carrying any medical information with him. He's not wearing any allergy tags. Please work with us here," the nurse stated curtly.

The same doctor who tended to Mandy was on duty. "Hello, Mr. Sullivan, how's the horse crazy girl doing?" They chatted briefly before Dr. Gardner got called away.

Big Dan walked to an empty counter and started taking out the contents of the man's wallet. A driver's license with an address he recognized – the VA hospital near Pittsburgh. Sears and visa credit cards. A military identification card. A faded photo of an old woman, $34 and a piece of paper with the first two verses of Psalm 91: *He who dwells in the shelter of the Most High will rest in the shadow of the Almighty. I will say of the Lord, He is my refuge and my fortress, my God, in whom I trust.* Big Dan knew that as the "Soldier's Prayer." His name was Lieutenant Colonel Paul Robert Silverton.

"He's a veteran," Big Dan told the nurse, who asked him to go to the registration desk, so at least they could begin a medical chart. Once he gave them all the information he knew, he carefully put the things back into the wallet and was instructed to hang on to it for him.

The Colonel had been sedated and moved to an operating room. Dr. Gardner came over to Big Dan. "Ruptured appendix," he quickly explained. "We're going in to drain it well and repair it. Another few minutes, and it's anyone's guess if he would have made it." Dan left his telephone number and headed home.

On the way, he decided to check on the horses at Amethyst Valley. He didn't know anything about horses, but he'd figure out something if necessary. He could always go get Mandy, Danny and Martha to help. State Highway 24 was no place for a loose horse.

The workmen were busy back at the fence when Big Dan swung into the driveway. A maroon Ford Explorer turned in just in front of him coming from the other direction, and they arrived at the house the same moment. An attractive woman in her mid-50s got out and looked Big Dan's way. She had a puzzled expression on her face, taking note of the chewed up porch plants, manure in the front yard and three horses in the arena, looking forlornly at the pasture.

"Do you know what's going on here?" she asked nicely in a smooth, Southern accent.

Big Dan relayed the events of the past hour, and she seemed instantly concerned and relieved. "Colonel Paul is my right hand man, my general manager. He lives in the cabin and watches over everything, as well as doing some horse training. I depend on him totally, and right now, I have no time to look after things. My mother has dementia and needs 24/7 care. I'm looking at care facilities; my husband is out of the country; and I work full-time. Since you're here in the middle of the day, is there any way you can help out until we find out what's going on with Colonel Paul? And, why did you stop by in the first place?" And then she quickly added, "I'll need some references, of course, and thank you already for taking him to the hospital and coming back to check on things."

"Ma'am, I've never been around horses. I don't know anything about them. I have a horse crazy daughter who sits on that hill every day and has watched everything get repaired and replaced and repainted. She updates us every night at dinner," he smiled. "I'm a mechanic and truck driver. I can fix anything, and I'm out of work right now. I stopped to see if you need more help with the fencing or any handy-type work when I found Colonel Paul. I was laid off from Morton's Machine Shop recently after seven years because of the slow economy. If you can show me what you want, I'll talk it over with my wife and see how we can help you out," he said, not considering any payment.

"Well, first of all," she stated, "we need to move these horses from the arena to the pasture and clean up both the arena and the front lawn. She set her purse and a monogrammed, canvas briefcase with the letters NBA in script on the hood of the Explorer." They walked to the barn, where she lifted some lead ropes off hooks.

"I suppose the fence workers just drove them into the first contained area they saw. Well, you're certainly a big fellow, and I'm going to give you a crash course in leading a horse. If your references check out, we'll go over what Colonel Paul does every day for horse feeding and turning out and returning them to the stalls for the night. You can do your best. It'll take a couple hours morning and less than an hour in the evening. I will pay you $100 a day. I'll call the hospital later. Will you go back and check on the Colonel, too? He came highly recommended as a manager and horse trainer. I think it's his first work position since nearly a year at the VA hospital for surgeries and rehabilitation. He was so certain he could do the work here. Now, I wonder."

Big Dan was taken aback momentarily. That was good money for a few hours of work. He made a mental note to thank Pastor Porter for praying with him and for him. He told the lady that Colonel Paul was holding his belly and didn't say anything about being kicked or knocked down by a horse. "The ER doctor said it was a ruptured appendix. I don't think it had anything to do with his mobility or work here." He didn't mention noticing the lower leg.

"Oh, I'm so sorry, I haven't even introduced myself. I'm Natalie Adams. This land and the horse farm are a life dream for me and my husband, Matthew. He's an international airline pilot, soon to retire thankfully. He'll be overseas most of the summer, then home for good in the fall. I plan to move my business home, and I am thinking about adding a small apartment for my mother if I cannot find a suitable care facility."

"I'm Dan Sullivan, ma'am. Mechanic, truck driver, married father of two – my horse crazy Mandy and son Danny."

While the two walked with the lead ropes to the arena to move the three horses, Mandy and Anne were stationed at the hilltop hideout on the old beach towel with the binoculars. Anne had seen Mandy's father twice, once at her house and once in church.

"Mandy, that looks like your father walking to the arena," she said.

"Don't be ridiculous, Anne, my father knows nothing about horses. Let me look. It's probably the limpy man maybe just not limping today."

Mandy raised herself on her elbows and put the binoculars to her eyes just as Big Dan copied Mrs. Adams by hooking the lead clip to the circle on the bottom of the halter. "Whaaaaat is Daddy doing there???" she cried out. "What's going on?"

She didn't know whether to run down the hill to the farm or back to the house. She watched for another couple minutes. Just in case her eyes were playing tricks on her, she decided to head for home, running cautiously. No more slips or broken arms. It was nearly summer. School would be out soon, and she planned to go to the farm to see if there was a job for her. Any job.

A Noble Spirit .

Chapter
8

Mandy and Anne burst into the Sullivan's back door, all breathless and talking rapidly at the same time. "Daddy's at the farm. Some lady was showing him how to lead a horse out of the arena," Mandy chattered. "It was Mr. Sullivan," Anne shouted. "I saw him first in the binoculars. He was walking with a woman to get the horses out of the arena, and they moved them to the pasture."

They stopped and looked at each other. The binoculars! The beach towel! The backpack! They forgot everything in their hurry to come home. Just then Mr. Sullivan drove in, and they flew out the front door clamoring at his driver's side door, once again talking at the same time and firing questions.

"Girls, girls, girls," exclaimed Big Dan. "Whatever are you talking about?" he asked with a smirk on his face and twinkle in his eye.

"We saw you," said Anne, "from the hilltop hideout with the binoculars." With that final word, the girls exchanged glances.

"And what about the binoculars?" he asked.

"In our excitement, Dad, we forgot to pick them up. The towel, the backpack, it's all still up there," Mandy explained.

"Well, sweet pea, what have I told you about borrowing something of value from someone?"

"That I am to take extra good care of it because it doesn't belong to me, and someone trusted me enough to loan it," Mandy responded quietly.

"Okay, I'll tell you all about it inside. After supper, we'll walk up the hill to get the stuff," Big Dan said, putting an arm gently around each girl's shoulders.

"Does your mother know where you are, Anne? Please call her. You are normally home by now," Martha instructed just as the phone rang. It was Kate. Martha assured her that all was well, and the girls lost track of time in the excitement of seeing Big Dan at the horse farm. If okay with Kate, Anne could eat supper with them. Then Big Dan and Mandy would walk back up the hill and walk Anne home to her back door.

"The girls left the backpack, beach towel and Dan's binoculars up there," she explained. "Anne has accepted partial responsibility and wants to go back with them to pick up everything." That was fine with Kate, and when Martha asked how she was doing, Kate said, "Very well, my friend. I'm feeling strong and really enjoyed being in church on Sunday. See you again soon."

Danny popped downstairs to find out about supper, and Mandy noticed Anne's face brighten with interest. She wanted to roll her eyes, but even she had to admit that her brother was quite the cutie at 16.

Martha set an extra place for Anne, and the five sat down to a spaghetti pizza dish and artisan bread that Martha had just learned to make. Anne loved it and asked for the casserole recipe. She was a little nervous being across the table from Danny, but they all sat in rapt attention as Big Dan relayed the series of events that brought him to leading horses from the arena to the pasture. While he didn't mention the amount of money, he said he could be working there part time for a few weeks, while Colonel Paul recovered, and his smile and nod to Martha signified that it was a good thing.

The phone rang again, and they could hear Big Dan saying, "yes, yes, that's good news. Oh, good. I'll be over soon."

Chapter 8

"That was the hospital," he reported. "Colonel Paul has come out of surgery in good shape, and he's asking who brought him to the hospital. The doctor said he'll be fine after a few weeks of rest, at least a month."

Mandy, Anne and Big Dan skipped dessert to go to the hilltop hideout. Danny went along, too, and on the way down the hill to the Dawsons, he asked Anne if she ever stayed after school for the baseball games. She said she'd ask her mom and let him know if she could do that some time. Mandy and Danny still had time for homework, and Big Dan headed for the hospital.

His visit with Colonel Paul was filled with gratitude. Both were men of few words, so conversation didn't roll along like it did with the girls or between Martha and Kate. Big Dan and Colonel Paul just sat there quietly, as men will, for half an hour. The prosthetic foot device rested on a chair nearby, and neither man mentioned it. When Big Dan said he met Mrs. Adams, and he could help at the farm until the Colonel was completely back on his feet, the bedridden man nodded a grateful smile.

He was a bit groggy, but did express concern about losing his job when he heard he would have a four to six week recovery. "I've already lost mine," stated Big Dan, explaining why he stopped at the farm in the first place, looking for work. "I met Mrs. Adams when I went back to check on those loose horses. I'll help out as best as I can for as long as it takes."

And there was more thankfulness by the patient for Big Dan's quick response. "Another 10 or 20 minutes, and the doctor said I could have died there. Because of your quick action, they got it drained and fixed. I can't quite imagine dying on a barn floor after two tours of duty and heavy combat in Afghanistan," he said as his eyes closed and he drifted off.

Big Dan set the wallet on the bedside stand, asked the nurse on duty if she thought he needed anything and said he'd be back the next afternoon. Mandy's father went home, tired and full of thankfulness himself, even if just for temporary work.

Mandy's arm healed quickly. She did all the strengthening exercises the physical therapist ordered, and Mr. Morton carried the family on his company's health insurance for two more months, which covered her medical expenses. She visited Noble every day, and Anne climbed on a few more times. She figured out how to slide off him, bend her knees slightly at landing and stay on her feet, most of the time.

They petted Noble, brushed him, combed his mane and tail, fed him apple and carrot pieces – not too many, Kate had warned them – sang to him and laid on the beach towel. They talked sometimes, and other times just drifted in their own thoughts as their friendship deepened. Mandy talked about the Wicked Three and how she wished she were not so tall. She wondered if she'd ever even have a boyfriend.

"Probably not," she decided, brightening up at her next thought. "I'll find a way to always have a horse, so I won't be lonely at all!"

Anne shared how much happier she was now that her mother could go out a little, and they were both making friends. "I wanted to be with her all the time so she wouldn't be frightened, and I felt if I made friends, I was deserting her. I think she needed me a lot when we first moved here, but now she's better, mostly because of your mother's friendship and encouragement. She went grocery shopping alone yesterday for the first time, and she saw one of the Bible study ladies there – I guess they sort of did a high five and whooped and celebrated her success in the produce aisle and a manager came over to see what was going on. Oh, hey, I almost forgot. Can you and your mom come over on Saturday afternoon in two weeks for our Kentucky Derby Day Party?"

"Every year," she continued, "we get silly, cheap hats – like at the dollar store or a garage sale - and decorate them with things we find outside – leaves, flowers, stones, feathers. We could come up here for acorns and pine cones, but it's a long walk. Anyway, we decorate our hats and wear them all afternoon. Mom cooks ribs and makes mint juleps with sparkling soda. We bake a Kentucky pecan pie the day before, and we just have a lot of fun! She and her sister, my Aunt Donna, started it when they were kids, so we have carried on the tradition."

Mandy asked if her aunt would come that day.

"No. Aunt Donna doesn't like us any more. Mom didn't say so, but I know. Last time we were at their house to look at apartments – we were going to move near them - I overheard my uncle and aunt talking about how to discourage us from moving to that side of the state.

They didn't know I was outside their open bedroom window getting the Frisbee from their dog. It's better here, I think, anyway, but I know Mom misses her sister. They picked a fight with Mom, and we had to pack our stuff and walk a couple miles to the bus station. We took the next bus back to my grandma's. Mom was pretty upset that Aunt Donna didn't come after us or even call to see if we made it home safely. We really like our little house – well, except for the color - and church and school. Please come for Kentucky Derby Day. It's silly, and we have lots of fun."

"I'll ask. Sounds like a good time, and I always watch the race," Mandy responded. Then she told Anne about her "Noble Spirit."

"I think of Noble when I'm sad about something or those girls come near me or I fight with my brother. Noble is always so gentle and calm, even though he doesn't have a horse friend in his pasture, and he is half blind. He's out here all night by himself, and he's always in a good mood and friendly. He holds his head up high and lets us sit on him. Noble can be our inspiration, Anne. I think he's incredibly full of courage. Just thinking of him makes me strong and happy, no matter what anyone says."

Anne smiled and squeezed Mandy's hand. "I need a 'Noble Spirit' sometimes, especially when someone asks about my father, and I don't have one."

As soon as she thought she could hold Noble's mane, Mandy decided to sit on him again. They bribed him to turn around and line up at the fence. Anne stood in front of him on the ground because Mandy didn't need her help to get on. She swung one long leg over him and pulled herself upright with his mane. She sat there for a minute, and then told Anne to move to the fence. Mandy had been reading the specifics of horseback riding every spare moment in recent weeks. The limpy man, well, Colonel Paul, had said that Noble was a finely trained horse.

Mandy let out her breath, forced her shoulders to sag a little and sink into her seat before she slightly squeezed her thighs. And she reminded herself to breathe. Noble moved off, stepping slowly while Mandy held on and adjusted herself to the side-to-side and front-to-back motions that coincided with his steps. He walked along near the fence for about 20 steps when a deer jumped up in the woods. Noble was startled and broke into a trot heading right for a large, fallen, oak tree!

Spaghetti-Pizza Casserole

~ Cook and drain one 8-oz
package of spaghetti
~ Spread noodles on bottom of
greased 9x13 glass dish
~ Cover with 1 cup shredded
mozzarella cheese
~ Mix together ¼ cup milk
and one egg; pour over cheese
~ Bake at 350° for 7 minutes;
remove from oven
~ Layer: ½ lb ground beef (cooked
and drained)
1 14-oz. jar spaghetti sauce
2 cups mozzarella cheese
~ Spread pepperoni on top
(one 6 oz. package)
~ Sprinkle with Parmesan cheese
~ Bake again at 350° for
30 minutes, uncovered.

Chapter
9

Mandy let out a yelp, then gathered her wits. Hang on, hang on, wrap your legs but not enough to press him into a gallop or anything that fast. She flashed on everything she read (keep breathing!) and prepared for the jump   or the fall. Noble moved from trot to canter effortlessly and smoothly lifted his front legs. His young rider leaned forward and stretched slightly backward from her seat, folded her knees at his sides and hung on. He sailed over the tree, landing gently and trotted to a stop. Mandy was still on!

Anne screamed with delight. Mandy took a breath, and let it out. Again. Once more. Noble stood still. She tried pressing her left leg only, and the gentle giant turned to the right. She kept on the pressure, until he turned 180 degrees and started walking back. Mandy steered him with her legs around the end of the fallen tree to where Anne kept her perch on the fence rail. Both girls were ecstatic!

"He can still jump," yelled Mandy. "What did it look like?"

"He looked perfect! You were a little sloppy, but you stayed on! Can I try it?" Anne asked, her eyes as big as saucers.

"That was an accident," Mandy reminded her. "Let's be careful up here. We don't want to get into any trouble. I am going to see if they have any summer jobs, and we're not supposed to be riding him at all." They knew they were pushing their luck by sitting on him every day, after checking that no one was coming or looking their way. Of course, in the past few days, they knew the farm manager wouldn't be around as he recovered from his unexpected surgery.

What they didn't know was that they weren't the only ones with a pair of binoculars. Colonel Paul had been watching them all along. He came home from the hospital that morning with Big Dan, and he saw the jump from his bedside window in the cabin.

Big Dan had been working at the farm a week now. Natalie Adams made a list of the basic morning and afternoon horse chores. She had drawn a sketch of the farm land and patiently went over everything the first morning. There were six horses in stalls every night, four outside in the north pasture and Noble in the high pasture. Two pastures were vacant at night, and she planned to rotate the horses regularly among the fenced areas.

"You can earn extra money digging out the thorns from that field," she said, pointing beyond the cabin. "You can toss them, roots and all, over there on the other side of the woods. I'm going to cut trails into that 110 acres going up the hill, lots of switchbacks, I'm sure. It's fairly steep, but it will make a nice climb. We'll put a gate at the top so riders can go across the top pasture and down the other side. Probably need another gate, but I haven't had time to think that far ahead."

Two of the outside horses needed supplements. Five of the six stalled horses got something, different grains or amounts and supplements for each one. Noble was on hoof supplement and pelleted rice bran mixed with water to make a daily mash. Big Dan made this and slid it under the fence for him every morning.

Natalie had everything extremely well-organized, with different colored scoops and bins and lead ropes for each horse. She had written notes about their personalities, and which one went into which pasture on her diagram. She also said she would move Apache early every morning, before leaving for work. "He's young, high strung and a bit full of himself. I'll feed and turn him out and put him away when I return each evening. The rest are fairly well-mannered horses. The most important element of horse handling is confidence; just lead them around like you know what you're doing. The four outside together over there are mine. One of the stalled horses is mine, and the other five are boarding."

Natalie told Big Dan as much as she knew about Noble. "He was given to me a year ago when a friend needed to find homes for three of her horses. He had been a blue ribbon show jumper before he lost sight in one eye in some pasture accident. No one seemed to know exactly what happened. He was used as a school horse for a couple years, and my friend thought he'd make a good companion horse or lesson horse when I got the farm up and running. Unfortunately, the other horses pick on him too much, so I separated them. He's got one of the sweetest dispositions I've ever seen, especially in a Thoroughbred. He deserves to be with someone who can spend time riding and enjoying him, so that's why he's for sale. For his benefit. He's 20."

She pointed out a garden area and a low spot she planned to have dredged and dug out for a pond. The first morning, they did all the feeding together, measuring and mixing grain and supplements, adding water to every dish for a mash serving. She instructed him again on leading each horse from the stall to the appropriate pasture. Once the horses were all outside, she picked up the manure rake and a bucket. "I think I can figure out this part, ma'am," Big Dan stated flatly. "And then I'll dig out those thorns. Thank you for the work."

Just as Mrs. Adams was leaving, she rolled down her Explorer window and said, "Dan, please bring down Noble a week from Thursday at 4:00. Some people are coming to look at buying him." And with that, she steered down the driveway and turned left on to State Highway 24. He went to work, thinking about whether or not to tell Mandy about another possible buyer for Noble.

Over lunch at home, he told Martha about it. "We may as well tell her, Dan. Life is full of disappointments and surprises. She's just a young teenager. She has her whole life ahead of her to follow her horse dreams. Didn't you say this was Natalie's life dream, this farm, and she must be on the other side of 50? It won't be easy, but it won't be any easier if someone buys him, and you knew about the people coming."

Big Dan nodded slowly, wishing there was a way, but no, there was no way. Two thousand dollars was way too much money for a horse, not to mention then having to pay a monthly fee and buy stuff like a saddle and lead rope and halter. That was all he figured a horse needed, but it was still not in their family budget, which was a bit tight these days.

When he told Mandy at supper about the folks coming to look at Noble, she just stared at him. Her lower lip trembled. She swallowed hard and asked to be excused, pushing away a half-eaten dinner plate and running upstairs to her room. The door closed quietly, and they heard the sobbing in the kitchen, even stifled as it was in her pillow.

Martha found two hats at a dollar store, one a plastic lime green and the other a basic straw hat, both with wide brims. Since Kate insisted on making all the food – "it's a tradition," she'd said, Martha put together a small basket of flavored tea and juices to take along. After a light lunch on Saturday, she and Mandy walked over to Kate and Anne's after visiting Noble. Like Big Dan, Martha would love nothing more than having the means to buy Noble for Mandy. They had some money in a savings account, but with her husband out of work, they might need it.

They went in through the back porch and found mother and daughter assembling glue, tape, old baskets, scissors and pruning shears. They foolishly ooh'd and aah'd over the hats and headed outside, gathering some tall grass, stones, pine cones and shrubbery pieces. Anne found a gray feather, and Martha was the first to unwrap bark off a fallen log, not a live tree. They spent the better part of an hour picking up things outdoors, and another hour gluing and arranging their hats.

Kate had printed a list of the horses racing, and they all chose a favorite based on total non-essentials like names and colors and stockings. They talked mostly about horses all afternoon, and Mandy's mom enjoyed listening and watching. The food was wonderful, and the race was, as always, very short. The whole event distracted Mandy from her concern about Noble possibly being sold on Thursday.

The next morning at church, they learned that Mrs. Porter's twins had been born the previous afternoon. Mandy tried to participate in her Sunday school class, but her mind now drifted to the horse. She still called him Gentle Giant sometimes, and when she went to the hilltop hideout on Monday, she prayed again.

"Dear God. It's Mandy again. Some people are coming next week to look at buying Noble. I see him almost every day, and he waits by the fence for me. I can tell that he's very happy. I am his best friend, and he is my best friend, along with Anne now. Dad has been giving him mash every day, and he says he's a very nice horse, and he doesn't know anything about horses. Oh, and please find him a job. He's really smart, God, even if he didn't go to college. He's a hard worker, too. Anyway, Gentle Giant gives me confidence and strength and I love him and I'm so afraid of losing him. Help me be strong and give me a really big 'Noble Spirit' please. Love, Mandy. Amen."

A Noble Spirit

Chapter
10

"Miranda! Miranda Sullivan! Are you here with us? Are you paying attention at all?" Mrs. Engels' voice boomed through Mandy's distress.

"Yes, no, yes, I guess not, I'm trying to p-p-pay attention," she stammered, tears welling in her eyes and spilling down her cheeks. The Wicked Three in the back of the classroom rolled their eyes and stifled giggles.

"Pull yourself together, and we'll talk after class," the teacher said sympathetically, as she directed her attention to the back of the room. "Amanda, Kerry, Jennifer, do you each have something you wish to contribute to this study of Beethoven?" When they shook their heads negatively in unison, she continued: "I want to see all three of you after I speak with Mandy. Wait in the hall after class."

The last 10 minutes dragged on, but finally the bell rang and everyone left the room except Mandy. The Wicked Three waited outside. After Mandy told Mrs. Engels that she wouldn't understand, the teacher said "try me," thinking it was about being made fun of for being tall. Mrs. Engels was six feet tall herself. Mandy told her about the horse she'd made friends with and how he gave her self-confidence and how tall he was and that he was alone from the other horses, like she felt at school sometimes, and that he might be sold next week, and she thought she'd die of a broken heart. She described the "Noble Spirit" and how she gained courage from the horse.

Mrs. Engels talked briefly about struggles with her height and about a puppy she got and lost at about the same age. "We survive these animal dramas, Mandy. Not easily, but we do. Trust me. You will be okay, if not this week or next, then during the summer." Mandy nodded and left. The Wicked Three said nothing this time when Mandy walked by them, and they approached Mrs. Engels.

"Girls," she began, "you are in a time of life where each one of you grows or develops or learns at a different pace. I've seen you making fun of Mandy for her height. I was a tall girl, too. She doesn't retaliate or shout insults at you or poke fun at your, um, pierced ears (she looked at Jennifer) or your bleached blond hair (she looked at Kerry, wondering whose mother would allow bleaching hair in ninth grade) or your short toes (glancing down at Amanda's sandaled feet). She has a burden right now, and she needs friends, not snickering classmates. I expect better from you all from now on."

They mumbled a respectful "yes, Mrs. Engels" and left the room, wondering what was the problem with Mandy. She had a great, solid family, and a cool, older brother. Inside, Jennifer really wanted to be her friend, but she didn't know how. Things weren't very happy at her house, and she was angry at the world because of it.

The following Thursday after school, Mandy climbed to the hilltop hideout. She just couldn't stay away, though she knew Noble would be in the arena at 4:00 for the people to look at. He was there already, just holding his head over the fence, looking at the grass and other horses nearby. She started crying, and she was sure that Noble looked up the hill at her.

A white SUV came into view, and a man, woman and two girls got out and walked to the arena. Mandy started walking downhill in the side woods. Big Dan greeted them and said that Mrs. Adams had an emergency with her mother and could not be there as she expected to be, but this was Noble, and they could walk into the arena. He left Noble's halter on and handed the father the lead rope. The dad hooked on the lead rope so the horse would stand still, and they all walked around him and touched him. He led Noble around the arena so they could see him move. The mother was the only one, it seemed, even to Big Dan, who was interested in the horse.

Mandy came running from the woods yelling at them. "You can't buy him! He's an awful horse! He won't do anything you want! He's half blind so he can't see anything on one whole side, and he doesn't know where to walk or go! And he's not very smart either!"

"Miranda!" shouted her father, stepping over to the running girl and stopping her securely with one big arm. "You are way out of line, young lady, and you apologize to this family this minute. Get a hold of yourself and tell them you are sorry," he commanded.

Before she had a chance to speak, Big Dan explained about the horse farm recently opening and his daughter befriending Noble and visiting him daily at the fence. Neither Mandy nor her father noticed Colonel Paul amble over, slowly shuffling his feet and leaning on a cane.

"Where's Colonel Paul?" asked the mother indignantly. "Mrs. Adams said he's the horse expert on the property."

"I'm Colonel Paul," the man said evenly, clumsily moving a few feet in front of Dan and Mandy.

"Well," the mother sniffed, "you're supposed to be some sort of horse guru, what do you think?"

Colonel Paul looked seriously at the two teenage girls who had hardly paid any attention to Noble. One replaced the iPod earphones the father told her to take off, and the other one was preoccupied with her lipstick and hair.

"Oh, this girl is right. Noble cannot see anything on his right, and he might step on something or stumble when you least expect it," Colonel Paul informed them.

"But Mrs. Adams said he has lots of training, and he'd be good for a beginning rider. I want my girls to take horseback riding lessons, and we can afford the horse," the mother insisted.

Colonel Paul, Big Dan and Mandy by now figured out the mother wanted the horse, not the girls. "I don't think he's the best horse for your lovely daughters," explained Colonel Paul. "I'm sorry you may have been misinformed."

With that, the dad released Noble, tossed the lead rope over the nearest fence rail and stomped back to the car. The mother put her nose in the air, and the girls, looking relieved, got back into the vehicle.

"Mandy, go home. We will discuss this later," her father said sternly. She respected his tone of voice and turned for the long walk home.

Mandy was grounded for one week, the last week of school. She had extra work at home to do cleaning and helping her mother, and she had to wash and vacuum her dad's truck and her mother's car. Anne could not come over, and she could not go to the hilltop hideout. It was the longest week of her life, and a million times she thought of her "Noble Spirit" and stayed strong.

School was out after a half day on Friday, and Mandy was free to go up the big hill once again. It was just after lunch, and she knew her father would not be at the farm yet to help with the afternoon chores. She left the binoculars and her backpack at home and walked to the top. Noble was not there. She looked all over the pasture, but it was empty. Her heart sank, and she got a knot in her throat.

"Where is he?" she cried. "Gentle Giant, Noble, Noble," she called, while her heart thumped in her chest. In a small pasture below where her father had removed thorns, she saw Noble lift his beautiful head, perk his ears and trot toward the upper fence when he heard her voice.

With a huge sigh of relief, she started toward him. In the same field, she saw a smaller, chestnut horse she had never seen. She couldn't see his face, but he had two white stockings on his back legs and one sock just above the front left hoof. He had a tail longer and thicker than Noble's and appeared to be the size and build of a mustang. A maroon Ford Explorer was parked near the house.

Noble nickered as she picked her way down the side of the pastures through the woods. It was dense and tricky to find places with good footing, but she had walked down a week ago - the day the family came to look at Noble - so she retraced her steps, winding back and forth on the steep parts, zigzagging like she did on the big hill behind her house. The difference here was all the fallen tree limbs, undergrowth and leaves.

Noble watched her and moved toward the side fence as she got closer. Mandy carefully slipped through the fence and walked up to him. "Noble, my gentle giant, here you are," she whispered into the side of his face, which he lowered next to her. The other horse moved away, then turned facing and watching her. Now she could see his thick mane falling on both sides of his neck, a wide, white blaze and cautious eyes. She thought that he looked sad and a little frightened.

"Oh, Noble, Noble. I couldn't find you, and I was scared. But here you are. Who is your new friend? Do you finally have a horse buddy? I brought these carrot pieces for you, my dear, wonderful, warm friend," she told him, slipping her fingers under his mane where it was always soft and warm. He leaned his forehead down to be stroked. "I can't get dirty. I'm going to see the farm owner. I'm sorry I haven't been here. I've been grounded, and I'll tell you all about it later."

She smoothed her plaid shirt, which was tucked neatly into a pair of tan capris and went back through the fence. She didn't see the limpy farm manager. One attractive woman was riding in the arena on a beautiful, caramel colored horse with a white star.

"Hi," Mandy called when the woman rode near the arena fence. "Your horse is beautiful. What kind is he or she?"

"She's a Morgan," the lady responded, riding to the fence and halting. "She's nine, and can you believe it? She's my first ever horse. I love her already like I've never loved anything!"

"Oh, I can understand that. She sure is pretty," Mandy said again. "Are you boarding here?"

"Yes, as of three days ago. I'm Margie White, and this is Harmony."

"Oh, are you a substitute teacher?" Mandy asked. When Mrs. White nodded her head, Mandy smiled at her. "I've seen you at school. You were in my music class a couple weeks ago when Mrs. Engels was sick."

"I was. I remember you, too. Nice to meet you again, is it ... Miranda?"

"Yes, but my friends call me Mandy, and that's good for you, too."

"Do you have a horse here?" asked Mrs. White.

Mandy told her about watching the horse farm from the top of the hill the past several weeks and making friends with Noble the Thoroughbred. "He's over there now," she pointed, "with another new horse, but he's always been in the high pasture right next to the fence where I have my hilltop hideout. It's really just an old towel I lie on, but it's become a really special place. Wow, that's two new horses in the week I was ... ah, away. I was grounded." She looked away for a moment. "But it's over now, and I'm going to see if there's any summer work here."

"Good luck," said Mrs. White. "I hope to see you around."

Walking up to the front door of the big house, she rang the bell and stood tall. A nice looking, older woman opened the door.

"I'm Miranda Sullivan," she began, "and my friends call me Mandy. May I talk to you about something important?"

"Of course," smiled Natalie Adams, knowing this was Big Dan's daughter. She heard about the recent outburst at the arena when the family came to look at Noble. "Let's sit on the back patio," and she led Mandy through a lovingly restored farmhouse to a slate floor patio with two tables, blue striped cushioned chairs and matching umbrellas. "Would you like a soda?"

"No, thank you," Mandy said. She pulled out an envelope from her pocket and took a deep breath. "I have loved horses all my life, and I read and learn everything I can about them. I know that when someone puts a price on a horse, like a truck or a boat, a person interested in buying makes an offer. Well, two thousand dollars is a whole lot of money. I thought if you don't really need that much money, maybe you would take an offer. I can give you a down payment and work and earn the rest. I'll be 15 at the end of the summer, and I babysit, or, um, maybe I can work here. I'd clean your house and sweep this patio or dig up thorns, like Dad did, or wash the horse trailers. I'll do anything, and I know how to work hard," she said, trying not to act desperate. "I saved my birthday money from last year, some from babysitting, and I earned a little helping a family pack to move. I have $64. You can have it all, and I'll make more, and I'll pay for Noble if it takes 10 years."

Natalie was quiet. She didn't need the money. She understood this young girl's heart, but there was one problem. "I would love to consider your offer, Mandy. But Noble was sold yesterday."

Chapter
11

Mandy braced herself and vowed not to cry. She thought of Noble's courage in the pasture alone day after day in all kinds of weather, and carrying on with just one eye, and she embraced her "Noble Spirit." Her lower lip quivered, and she sat up straight to keep from folding, then started to get out of her chair.

"Thank you, anyway," she began to say, just as Mrs. Adams continued. "Mandy, Colonel Paul bought him. A horse from Fort Bragg Army Base arrived a few days ago for him, and the Colonel didn't want the new horse – his name is Cash - to be alone when he arrived in a strange place. He thought Noble would be the perfect, calm pasture companion that a newly displaced horse might need. He has a lot of work responsibilities and horse training to do here managing the farm, the boarders and now the new horse. Your dad said you love horses, and you wanted to quit school and work here, which, of course, you cannot do. But it's practically summer, are you out of school yet?"

"Today was the last day, and I haven't seen Noble in a week. I was grounded because I behaved badly here last week when the people came, and ..."

"I know, Mandy, I heard about it." Mrs. Adams leaned forward smiling warmly. "Your father seems to think you can help Colonel Paul over the summer with some horse chores in exchange for learning to ride and care for Noble."

Mandy started laughing and crying and flew across the table to hug Mrs. Adams, knocking over the umbrella and just catching the glass table as it tilted toward the stone floor. "Oh, thank you, thank you," she cried and laughed, stabilizing the table and turning to go.

"Mandy. You might need this for boots or a helmet," she called after her, handing her the envelope with the money.

Her dad's truck was in the driveway when Mandy emerged from the house, but she didn't see him around. She walked to the cabin and knocked on the door. "Come in," said Colonel Paul. Her father and the Colonel, whom Mandy never again referred to as the limpy man, were sitting at the wooden kitchen table with some papers and photos spread out. Mandy was instantly impressed with the little cabin. It was neat and clean and quite inviting. They asked her to sit with them.

While showing them the photos, Colonel Paul told her and Big Dan about growing up in south Texas, where he learned to ride and train horses and speak Spanish at a young age. "Most of the trainers were brutal, but I learned that horses respond to leadership techniques and body language in a positive way. Once trust has been established, a horse will try very hard to learn whatever you teach it. They were more dependable than most of the people I met as a kid," he said.

"There was no future there, no jobs, nothing for me, so I joined the Army when I was 18," he continued. When they discovered his extensive experience with horses, he was stationed at Fort Bragg, N.C., home of the airborne and special operations forces and one of the Army's stables of horses. He talked about teaching army troops to catch, halter and tack a horse, how to mount and ride, tie and care for a horse.

"In remote and rocky terrain where jeeps can't go, horses and donkeys are the only mode of transportation in places like Afghanistan. Our elite troops are not generally well-trained in horsemanship, so that was my job. We'd also teach basic care and elementary vet skills, so they could help local farmers in rural communities with sick animals or herd and pasture management. It helps develop trust and goodwill to connect this way with the locals over there," he explained.

Colonel Paul told them about being deployed twice to Afghanistan and the improvised explosive device that took his left foot and part of his ankle and saved some of his buddies, and for which, they learned later, he was awarded the Purple Heart. It was the most he'd talked in a long time, and he simply asked for their confidence and no pity. "No one needs to know this stuff," he ended, gathering up the photos and putting them into a worn, manila envelope. "I can prove myself here – to myself and to Mrs. Adams, who has trusted me with the farm management." Then he turned to Mandy.

"About you and Noble," he began. Then he stopped. He looked at her bright, young, innocent eyes, which had grown wider with the reference to Noble. He looked at Big Dan and back at Mandy. "I've seen you up there, ah-hem, petting the gentle giant, as you call him. How would you like to work here in exchange for learning to take care of him and, ah, ride … and maybe jump, ah, if you don't already know how."

At that moment, she knew that he knew. She didn't know how, but she decided right then and there that Colonel Paul was not a man to keep a secret from. He'd just shared his with her and her dad. She smiled. "Yes, I'd love to work and learn. I need to check with my parents, and I'm willing to work hard for the privilege, sir."

"Already done, little lady. Your parents have agreed. And don't call me sir. You can call me Colonel Paul. We'll begin Friday at 10 a.m., three days a week, Monday and Wednesday also. I have work for you, and I will teach you horsemanship skills, horse care and basic riding, and maybe some small jumping," he said raising one eyebrow. "Mrs. Adams is going to put together a work agreement with how much you get paid and what we exchange."

"Oh, and one more thing, Mandy," he said, once Big Dan was out of earshot. "Do not get on Cash. He's come here because he's too spooky for the Army. Most of the troops are not experienced horse people, so all the Army horses need to be calm and nearly bombproof. Somehow, Cash got donated to them without the proper background check. They didn't know anything about his history except that he is about 22, he's a work horse/pony cross – looks Belgian to me - and the previous owner said he has a choking problem. Anyway, a buddy of mine at the base called to say I can have him, so they trucked him over four days ago. He's shy or scared, probably both. Anyway he's too jumpy for them to use for training, so he's now mine. He's a handsome fellow, and I'm not sure what his problems are, but for now, steer clear until we know more. I think it's going to take some work to win his trust."

Mandy promised, remembering how sad Cash looked to her. On her walk back home, she went through the fence again, petting Noble while Cash looked on from his safe distance.

Mandy showed up promptly at 9:55 a.m. Friday and began the summer learning about safety around horses. Colonel Paul explained about their dual eyesight, viewing an image from each eye on each side of their head, and how they cannot see directly in front or behind them. Of course, Noble could only see about 160 degrees on the left. She learned how to put on a halter, clip the lead rope, never wrap a lead rope around a hand or finger, walk Noble calmly and tie a quick release knot, all on the first day.

He also brought her to each horse and introduced them. She was right about the white Arabian, whose name was Kazi. "Short for T.D. Kaszandra," Colonel Paul said. "She's 14.2 hands – know what a hand is?" he asked. Mandy nodded. She knew exactly how to measure a horse, including how to calculate weight from girth and length measurements. "We'll she's 20 and has won blue ribbons in trail competitions and a trophy for English halter. She's the alpha mare in this herd – and you know what that means?" Mandy nodded.

"Mrs. Adams bought her at age 9 with no training. She and her daughter, Diane, trained and showed her. She's had three foals, and Natalie says that 'until you've seen her run full out with her tail flagged, head high and nostrils flaring, you haven't witnessed one of nature's most spectacular creations.' You watch, Mandy. You'll see her like that one of these days, and indeed, she is spectacular!"

The bronze and creamy Appaloosa belonged to her other daughter, Summer. Her name was Paloosa, and she was 12 years old. The girl did all her training and mostly rode and jumped her bareback since the horse was

5, though she could ride and show in both English and Western classes. Diane was married and lived in another state. Summer was a sophomore in college.

"Mr. Adams is an international airline pilot, and he arranged to spend the summer near their daughter, Summer, who's attending a year abroad school program in Switzerland. When she's not studying and her dad is not flying, apparently they're bumming around Europe together."

Natalie got the Rocky Mountain two years ago for her husband. His name was Monty, short for Montana Dream. "He's 10," Colonel Paul said, "and will mostly go for trail riding. The palomino is her horse, a Spanish mustang named Liberty Belle, with an e on Belle. She just calls her Belle. She is 9 and also trained Western for a trail horse. I think she said she showed in Western Pleasure classes last year. She has had her since she was born and she's had one foal. She's planning to breed her again next year."

"Two of the bays in the next pasture," he continued, walking to and through the next gate, "are boarded show horses. The large one with the thin blaze is a young Dutch Warmblood gelding named Apache. He's almost 4 and quite spirited. A trainer works with him three times a week, and his owner, Rachel, is just 18. If you ask me, which no one does and it's not my business anyway," he said near a whisper, "he's way too much horse for her. The pony, Checkers, belongs to her, too. He was her first pony. He's 21, I think. Nice, calm pony, probably some Welsh in him."

The one with the star was a Trakehner named Star of the Eastern Sky. Her owner was an experienced dressage rider, and Mandy had seen her many times in the arena. The other bay was a Tennessee Walker-Thoroughbred cross named Viking, and he also belonged to Natalie. He was an all-around English and Western trained horse which had been shown, jumped, ridden in parades and on trails. He was diagnosed last year with navicular disease and wasn't ridden much any more. Colonel Paul gave him a little extra attention. He didn't know how old he was, maybe around 18, he thought.

The buckskin horse, Darcy, was 10 and belonged to a restaurant owner who mostly did trail riding, camping and endurance rides. "She's a Quarter Horse, and the man who owns her also raised and trained Poko, this Quarter Horse cross. He is 26 and goes on short trail rides. He's happy to have them closer to his business. That Adams trailer over there with the small living quarters in the front and blue trim is his," said Colonel Paul pointing beside the barn.

"And now with Cash and Harmony, plus Noble, we have 13 horses, four vets and three different farriers, if you count me. I'll take care of Cash and Noble's feet most of the time. You may walk up to all of them, except Apache. He's unpredictable, and Cash probably won't let you get close to him. The others are nice. Do not take any treats to them – their owners give them enough, and it's not our place to do that. You can visit and pet them when you have time. Remember everything I said about approaching a horse. Always let them see and hear you coming. Walk to their shoulder area, and don't look directly at their eyes. If a couple of them are close together, never mind. You never know when the boss horse is going to spur another to move, and you could be in the way. It'll take you a little while to get comfortable with them and them with you, so go slowly. And never, never forget to close a gate."

He taught her how to put fly spray and a fly mask on Noble, too. She paid attention to everything, doing chores exactly as assigned. She cleaned all the stall water buckets and filled them with clean water and returned them to the stalls. She swept the center aisle of the barn every day she was there, cleaned the little bathroom and mucked Viking's stall. The other boarders took turns shoveling their own and each other's stalls. Then she went outside and checked the outdoor water tanks, moving hoses and filling them twice a week, and emptying them and wiping them all clean on Fridays before refilling.

Mrs. Adams had a short list each week – cleaning the horse trailer and her truck or her SUV sometimes. Every week she swept the front porch and back patio, wiping the chairs, tables and railings before watering the flower pots. Mandy loved everything and thought it was the best place in the whole world.

She saw Mrs. White every time she was there. "I can't wait until those trails are finished," she'd say with a smile from her gorgeous Morgan.

Mandy learned how to bring Noble into the barn, settle him in the cross ties and groom him. Colonel Paul gave her a new clear, plastic, zipper bag with purple trim. In it were two brushes, a curry comb, a regular comb and a hoof pick. She loved leading Noble and brushing out the last of his winter coat until his dark brown coat glistened in the sun when they walked back outside.

The riders, instructors and trainers used the arena and round pen. Some lunged in the vacant pasture. Five horse trailers were parked beside the barn, and the tack room was filled with the aroma of leather, wood, hay and horse. Mandy looked at all the beautiful saddles and bridles and blankets.

As Mandy learned and worked, Colonel Paul got stronger, and Big Dan's responsibilities dwindled. He had not given up on finding a regular job, still driving to companies even farther from home for something full time, permanent. Natalie Adams was impressed with his quiet manner and diligent work ethic. He suggested taking down a couple of large, dead trees that might have fallen in a storm and injured a horse or a fence or a building. He brought his own chain saw, dropped them neatly out of the way and cut and stacked all the wood near Colonel Paul's cabin. She often noticed him taking a tool from his truck to tighten a hinge or hammer back in a nail that worked its way out.

Natalie was paying him for trail cutting, too. She drew a rough map of switchback trails through the woods along one side, then said she'd have two gates delivered so riders could go across the top pasture and out the other side. "It'll be a big circle, so no one has to back track," she said. "Go along and use your own judgment on where trails go naturally when you're in there and see the lay of the land, the trees and underbrush."

He loved working outside, and he didn't mind working alone at all. He had lunch a few times with Colonel Paul in his cabin. He enjoyed hearing his stories, and for Colonel Paul, it was nice to have someone to talk to. Being in the Army means you're never alone, and he'd only recently realized that he was a little lonely for human companionship. When that emotion struck him, he instantly went to work with Cash, to win his trust, even if just walking into the pasture and standing silently near by. He was a very patient man. One afternoon, Cash took a step toward him. Colonel Paul didn't move, neither did Cash again that day, but it was progress.

A Noble Spirit

Chapter 12

Big Dan told him over lunch one day about meeting Martha at the prison. "I'd probably still be there, on the other side of the bars, if it weren't for her," he said. "I was visiting my father, who was in prison more of his life than not. Martha was touring with her high school class – partly, I think, as a deterrent to committing any crimes that might result in prison time, and, in her case at least, as a learning experience. She was thinking of going to college for a degree in criminal justice. She didn't study it, though. She majored in fashion design instead, and, truth be told, she makes more money than I do. She's quite creative, and every dress is different. She has done a couple gowns for television actresses; I don't remember their names."

He told Colonel Paul about stealing cars for the fun of it. "I could hot wire anything when I was 10," he said with a smirk. "It was just a challenge. And I remember it was fun, at the time. Now that I know the cost of a car, I can't imagine looking out my window and finding my truck gone, and some kids have gone joy riding in it. Everything I got into trouble for was erased when I turned 18, and I had to decide which side of those prison bars I was going to live on."

"When I saw Martha again that summer at the state park beach, we remembered seeing each other before. We talked and started dating. She went to college, and I worked for a year to save money for truck driving school. I did that and drove over the road for two years with Old Dominion. It's a lonely job, so I asked to transfer to the local routes, even though it didn't pay as much. Anyway, Martha and I got married two weeks after she graduated. She's a preacher's daughter, and I think privately they hoped she'd marry a missionary or at least a pastor. We get quite a kick out of telling people we met in prison."

Two of the boarders contracted with Big Dan to haul horses for them using their rigs when they found out he was an experienced truck driver, and Mr. Morton called a few times for deliveries. But it was not steady work.

Natalie approached him on the last day of his daily work turning out and feeding the horses, for which she faithfully paid him $100 per day every week and extra for digging up the thorns and cutting trails. She was generous.

"I'm getting a couple bids on an apartment addition for my mother going off the back of the house on the right side," she said, handing Big Dan a sketch. "I'd be happy to have you submit a proposal if you're interested."

He took the paper and looked at the drawing, turning it to one side so he was viewing it as it would appear from the side. He asked a couple questions about materials and windows and how she envisioned that it would interface to the house. She suggested that he look at the drawing and come back on Saturday.

"I can show you which wall will be knocked out and how we think the apartment should flow," she said. He took the page and assured her that he would work on the trails every day for the next couple weeks, as long as it took. He even found himself looking forward to seeing the horses every day.

Danny overheard his parents talking about the bid for the addition at Amethyst Valley's farmhouse. "I don't know much about plans and bidding, Martha," his dad was saying. "I can build as nice an apartment as anybody, and I can figure the costs and some labor figures, but I don't know how to go about doing the proposal part or formal drawings. The county may want lots of paperwork and real drawings for the building permit."

"I can help, Dad," said Danny, stepping into the kitchen. "I can do some drafting on the computer, and my friend, Assan, is a whiz at CAD. He can help us. I know how to make a spread sheet. We learned it in school last year. I've been thinking about something else, too. I have my driver's license, and I'm tired of my summer job at the lake. It doesn't start for another couple weeks, and they won't have any trouble replacing me. What do you think about opening our own trucking service? We could buy Mr. Morton's old truck cheap, the one that didn't sell, and fix it up. I can paint our name on it: Sullivan & Son Trucking Company. It wouldn't cost much to start, and I can contribute the money I've saved. Or, maybe it should be Sullivan & Son Construction, if we build the apartment addition."

He'd been a lifeguard for the last two summers. It was fun being outside, and there were girls, but it was boring with lots of sitting and watching. He longed to do something more challenging, something on his own, not work for someone else. He was just waiting for an opportunity to talk to his father about his ideas.

"One thing at a time, son," his dad said. "Let's look at this sketch and see what you can do. We can go over Saturday to look at the walls and note exactly where she wants it. I'll do some research, start a list of materials and price them at the lumber yard and hardware store. Show me how the spreadsheet works, and if we get the job, we'll work on it together and see how things go. Ask your buddy Assan if he can go with us Saturday if he's good at drawings."

Two and a half weeks later, they presented a package of drawings, costs and explanations to Natalie Adams, and she agreed to let them build the addition for her mother. It's like she had already decided, since she had opened accounts they could use at both the lumberyard and hardware store. Danny and Assan, however, found lots of less expensive places to buy nails, hardware and supplies online – cheaper even with added shipping costs.

Kate's mother came for her and Anne the first two weeks of summer, so Mandy didn't see her until mid-June, a couple weeks before the 4th of July parade - the one with the horses from the next county's horse club. She had already told Anne all about it and the horses she had seen last year. "Oh, I hope they come this year!" Anne had exclaimed.

Anne got back home on a Tuesday, and she called Mandy right away. They agreed to meet in 15 minutes at the hilltop hideout. "I have so much to tell you," Mandy said excitedly.

As they flopped down on the old beach towel, propped on elbows, gazing at the horse farm below, Anne noticed right away that Noble wasn't there.

"Where is Gentle Giant? Was he sold?" she asked in a very concerned voice.

"He's over there, in the lower pasture with the smaller reddish-chestnut horse," Mandy pointed. "And yes, he was sold, Anne. To Colonel Paul!! He's not leaving the farm, and I'm learning to handle him, and I'm learning to ride! I'm working at the farm three days a week, too. And Colonel Paul is amazing. Let's not ever call him the limpy man again. But first, tell me about your vacation."

"It was sooooo cooooool, Mandy. I went on four horseback rides on the horses at the dairy farm down the road from where Mom grew up. The farm is in the same family, different horses, of course, and there were two boys about my age," she rolled her eyes. "They showed me how to lead and brush and even saddle Springer, an old Haflinger pony with a beautiful blond mane and tail. He was the perfect size for me, much smaller than Noble, that's for sure. We walked around the house and down a short path and through a creek and back. That was the best part of everything. I went shopping twice with my Grandma. She's really neat. Mom saw some of her old high school friends, too. It was fun to be there, but I think we were both really ready to come home, now that we have a real home."

Mandy told Anne all about visiting Mrs. Adams and her job and riding lessons. "And Mrs. White, the nice substitute teacher, do you know her? Well, anyway, she has a beautiful Morgan horse at the farm, and she's there every day. She is so nice."

"I know who she is," Anne said. "She taught geography when Mrs. Arseno had her baby."

They watched Colonel Paul walk for Cash, who kept walking away from him. The horse would stop and look at him. Colonel Paul also stopped and appeared to be talking to Cash. He looked at the ground, intentionally lowered his inside shoulder and walked toward Cash's shoulder. At about four feet, Cash would step away. After about 15 minutes of this, the man was able to stand next to him. Gently he slid a lead rope over Cash's neck and stood still. After a couple minutes, he slowly put on a halter and lead him to the round pen.

"What is he doing?" she asked Mandy, watching Colonel Paul force Cash to trot around the edge of the round pen.

"Well, horses are fearful animals – they're born that way - because they are prey animals, not predators. They don't eat other animals, but bears and cats – big ones, of course, like mountain lions – will attack and kill horses. They are herd animals and need other horses to be happy, or at least one. I was sad for Noble that he lived alone, but now he has Cash. In any herd, one horse is the leader, and he or she bosses around the other horses by making them move. Colonel Paul says if you control their feet, you control their mind, because it means you are the boss," Mandy explained. "Now, see, Anne, Colonel Paul is making Cash run circles, change directions, and when he stops and lowers his head and shoulders slightly in the center, Cash will slow down – eventually, well, he's still going around, but he will slow down. Then he should walk toward the center, but not right up to a person, a few feet away. There. See. He's walking toward Colonel Paul."

Anne picked up the binoculars to get a closer look. "Colonel Paul is walking away and around, and the horse is following him. That's so amazing."

"He's been doing this almost every day since Cash arrived," Mandy added. "At first, it took him an hour to catch him, but every day, it's shorter. Then you'll see him pick up a plastic bag or white rag or parka and let Cash see it and smell it. The first few times, Cash backed up or even spooked and ran to the other side of the pen, but now he lets Colonel Paul rub him all over. It's desensitization, and Colonel Paul says that Cash will get used to these things, and he'll get over his fear about them."

Mandy went on telling Anne about Colonel Paul riding Cash in the ring and in the arena a couple times. "The horse is nervous and fearful, but he's not at all mean. He doesn't bite or kick or do anything but walk or run away. He figures that Cash was abused, and that's why he doesn't trust humans. He says Cash obviously has had extensive training by the way he moves and responds, and maybe that's why they thought he'd be good in the Army. He's just real jumpy, and he sweats sometimes while standing still with Colonel Paul sitting in the saddle. He's scared. I think he always looks sad. Colonel Paul is very patient and nice to him. He says he'll get over it and make a great trail horse. He sure is beautiful. He has the thickest tail of any of the horses."

Anne met Mandy the next morning and went to the farm with her, just following and watching everything she did. They checked first with Colonel Paul that she could follow Mandy and watch or help, and they assured him that Anne would not be any problem. When the chores were done, they were allowed to bring Noble into the barn to brush him. They took him into the arena when no one was there and took turns walking him on the lead rope. When Colonel Paul came, they went back to the barn, and he supervised Mandy putting on a saddle and bridle, and they all walked back to the arena.

Mandy tightened the cinch again, like he had shown her the previous week, and walked him to the mounting block. She found the saddle to be hard and cold and stiff, compared to Noble's warmth when she was on him bareback. She loved feeling him move, and she swayed more with his motion and muscles than she could in the saddle. But, she followed Colonel Paul's instructions and learned quickly.

Of course, having a fully trained horse under her made everything fairly simple. Noble seemed to anticipate her every thought and would walk and stop and trot and walk and stop at about the same moment she was thinking of giving him a signal. Like any well-trained horse, he sensed the slightest change in her seat or hands – or even thoughts, it seemed.

Colonel Paul told her that he was not a professional riding instructor. He could teach her the basics, and at some point, she would probably want to take real lessons. She was a natural for balance, and she posted to Noble's trot having watched Internet videos and read all about horseback riding with good form. And it sure felt more natural to rise and fall with his trot than to sit and bounce through it.

That night, Anne urged her mother to begin driving past the grocery store and to the farm to see the horses and see her groom Noble and lead him in the arena. "I'll try, honey, really I will," Kate said.

Chapter
13

Kate invited the Sullivans and the Porters over on the 4th of July since the parade went down Newport Street right in front of her house. The Sullivans walked up the hill and down the other side to the brilliant blue dwelling around 1:00. The Porters all arrived soon after with the new twins sound asleep in a double stroller. While Big Dan, Danny and the pastor repaired a broken hinge on the garage door and stationed the grill away from the house, Martha and Kate set the outdoor table. Beverly stayed busy supervising her four youngest children. Anne, Mandy and Emily Porter moved chairs to the side of the street for the best in parade viewing.

"Oh, I forgot to tell you: Colonel Paul knew all along that we were sitting on Noble up there," Mandy told Anne. "He even saw that time he jumped over the tree! He's so nice and very smart about horses. I'm sorry I ever thought he was mean."

"He seems very patient and quiet. I like him, too," Anne said, as the first marching band rounded the corner a couple blocks away. Everyone else joined them, and Mandy thought Anne would faint when Danny took the chair next to her.

It was typical, small-town America, Independence Day parade fare: marching bands, a couple clowns and one on stilts, old cars honking and people waving, Girl Scouts, Boy Scouts, a couple politicians and a dozen floats, two ponies walking with the 4-H Club, and finally, four horses with a banner on one that read "Garrison County Horse Club".

There were three girl riders and one boy - all older teenagers, Mandy thought. Their horses were shiny and smooth. Their hooves looked like they had shoe polish on them except the one wearing red boots which matched a red and white saddle blanket. Mandy had never seen boots on a horse. Two had their manes braided with ribbons in their tails, and the others had fancy saddles. One had a leather flag holder with a large American flag anchored in it, which the rider held with her left hand.

"We need a horse club," Mandy suggested. "We don't have horses, but we can make a club anyway, and maybe some girls with horses will join."

"Just girls?" grinned Danny.

Mandy and Anne exchanged glances. "Anyone who loves horses can join," said Mandy. "Not snakes." Kate overheard them and volunteered to organize something, since she had been in one as a teenager. They agreed to ask everyone at the farm and some girls from school and church. The only requirement would be that you love horses.

Two church groups on hay wagons drawn by tractors followed the horses, then two guys with Newfoundland dogs pulling carts, a small military band with a veteran's group and the requisite, shiny fire trucks and emergency vehicles with sirens blaring.

After the parade, the guys grilled hamburgers and hot dogs, and they all hung out in the backyard eating and laughing. Kate made a red, white and blue cake like a flag with strawberries, blueberries and white gumdrops. The Porters and Mandy's family played kickball against the side of the garage. At one point, Mandy and Anne took Emily and her younger brothers and sister to the hilltop hideout. Mandy carried the 4-year-old half the way up, and they all crammed themselves on the old beach towel and looked at the horses.

"Some day maybe we can ride in a parade," she shouted to the gentle giant before picking up the towel to head back down. Noble lifted his head and looked up from his new pasture at the sound of Mandy's voice.

Kate printed information and some of her ideas for a horse club, and she, Anne and Mandy sat around the little back porch table a couple days later.

"First of all, we need a name," said Kate. They could use the name of their county, but that looked like they were copying the one in the parade. They thought of Amethyst Valley Horse Club, but maybe some of the members would have their horses at home or at another farm. And they'd have to ask Mrs. Adams first.

"Can we call it The Noble Spirit Club?" suggested Mandy. "Or Noble Spirit Horse Club?"

Kate smiled. "Anne told me about your 'Noble Spirit', and I think that's the perfect name and the perfect theme for the group. What do you think, Anne?"

"I love it," Anne replied.

Kate suggested that they think about writing a mission statement, which would be the purpose of the club, and then some activities they could do in the community or on their own, with or without horses. In just a couple hours, they formed the first ever "Noble Spirit Horse Club". They wrote a mission statement: "to promote an understanding of good horsemanship principles; to have fun learning about horses and their importance in history and today; and to exhibit a 'Noble Spirit' in our lives." They might change it later, but it was a beginning.

They decided anyone who loves horses can join, and they would have some activities throughout the year, maybe at least four. They decided to wait until they invited some girls – they didn't figure any boys would join, at least not right away – to decide what the club should actually do besides learn all they could and talk about horses. They made a list of ideas to bring up at the first meeting: bake sale, parade, volunteer, horse clinic, maybe a vet would come and talk to them – and bring a horse!

Kate said she'd make little flyers, and they could put them up on the bulletin board at church, the grocery store, hardware store, community center. Natalie Adams had just hung a bulletin board in the barn the previous week.

"We'll post one there, too," exclaimed Anne. "Mom, you have to come to see the farm and the horses. Can you drive that far yet? Can you at least try?"

Kate immediately kept her apprehension in check. "Maybe soon, Anne, maybe next week," she added optimistically. She was determined to drive around, at least in town, to the horse farm and church. Already she went grocery shopping whenever they needed something, and the more she did it, the better she felt about herself.

Anne met Mandy at the hilltop hideout on Mondays and Wednesdays to go to the farm with her. She had art lessons on Fridays, her grandma's summer gift. After Mandy's work was done, they watched riders in the arena or brought down Noble for grooming or just brushed him in the pasture. Cash was still too frightened to come near them, though he stayed closer and closer as the days went by, and most of the time, he would stand or just back up one step or two when Colonel Paul came to get him.

One day, Mandy held a piece of apple as far outstretched as her arm would go. She stood very, very still and looked at the ground in front of Cash so not to look him in the eyes. Just as her arm was getting tired, Cash took a few steps forward, stretched his neck as far as it would stretch and took the apple. He didn't move his feet back away, but stood there chewing the apple and looking sad. Mandy would ask Colonel Paul if she could brush Cash in the pasture if he would let her.

Colonel Paul continued instructing Mandy as well as he could, and she would bring him pictures from books and magazines and ask him to tell her if her ear and shoulder, hip and heel were lined up. They sort of patched together the riding lessons. Once he saddled Checkers, the pony, for Anne, showing and teaching her everything he did, then leading her around the arena. The second time, he let her walk him around the arena slowly by herself.

The time he spent with Mandy and Anne meant he had to work longer in the day, but it was summer. The days were long, and he had always enjoyed teaching horsemanship and basic riding at the base. They were also respectful girls, and he appreciated that. Mrs. White said she'd dismount and supervise, too, if he needed to do other things.

She wasn't an expert horsewoman, but she was sensible and great with kids, and she had taken riding lessons over the past two years.

Almost every day, even days when she didn't go to the farm, Anne asked her mother to try driving out there. It was only two and a half miles on the road, a little shorter over the big hill, of course. Kate started over there once. She turned off Newport Street and drove two blocks past the grocery story when she panicked and turned around. Safe once again at home, she chided herself for not pushing harder. She felt so stupid. It wasn't very far, but something about being in an unfamiliar place scared her.

Then one day Martha said she was going out to pick up Mandy for a dental appointment. Kate asked if she drove to Martha's house, could she follow her to the horse farm. It would be easier for Kate knowing someone was close to her, but she'd experience driving her own car. Then Anne could ride home with her.

So, off they went after lunch, driving in tandem from Mandy's house, past the grocery store and on to State Highway 24. They turned in at the Amethyst Valley Horse Farm sign and followed the winding, gravel driveway to the parking area next to the barn. Anne was giddy with delight. She grabbed her mother's hand and pulled her all over, showing her the arena, the barn, the horses, Checkers, the pony, the tack room. Kate was warmed by great memories of her own horse experiences.

As they rounded the barn at the far end, Kate practically collided with Colonel Paul, who was leading Apache into the barn. They sort of grabbed at one another, half stumbling, and the horse spooked and took off.

A Noble Spirit

Chapter
14

"I'm so sorry," Kate said at the same time as Colonel Paul. "I'll get the horse. This was all my fault. Anne was showing me around, and I was enthralled with all of it, the smell, the wood, the horses, the barn." She was a pretty young woman in a youthful pony tail, stonewashed jeans, lightweight boots and a red and white striped shirt.

She walked toward Apache about 20 feet away. He backed away, then turned and stepped sideways on the lead rope, startling himself. Kate gently spoke to him and reached for his lead rope. She ran her hand smoothly down his leg and lifted his foot off the rope. She stroked his neck, all the while speaking softly, and walked him to the barn. "Which stall?" she asked Colonel Paul.

"Over here," he said. "Where did you learn to handle a horse like that?"

"Oh, I lived near a farm and spent half – or more – of my time there when I was a kid. And I went to horse camp twice. I'm taking online classes with Penn Foster College for an associate degree as a veterinary technician. That's all," she responded, shrugging her shoulders.

As he closed the stall latch, he said "I'm Paul Silverton; they call me Colonel Paul. I'm the general manager here."

"Kate Dawson, Anne's mother. I've heard amazing things about you and your way with horses. Thanks a lot for your kindness to let Anne come with Mandy. I hope she has not been in the way," Kate said.

At that moment, Martha and Mandy appeared. "I'm leaving now, Kate, to take Mandy to the dentist. Are you comfortable? You sure did catch that horse easily," Martha said.

Kate said she was fine, and Anne would go home with her a little later. She felt safe in this place. Colonel Paul asked about her riding experience, and they chatted for 15 minutes about horses from their youth. Somewhere in Mandy and Anne's conversations, he picked up that Anne didn't have a father and that Kate was having some problem driving to the horse farm. He figured he'd just wait patiently for a time to suggest a short horseback ride. Such a proposition would take some courage on his part – a whole different kind of courage than he possessed, he realized quickly.

Two weeks passed. Kate stopped at the farm once again, this time driving alone. Anne so much wanted her mother to see her riding Checkers. She was watching Mandy ride Noble when her mom's green Mercury Sable appeared. She ran to the car when she saw her. "You did it, Mom! You're here. Are you okay? How was it?"

"Well, I almost turned around twice, but I kept coming, and, yes, here I am." She kissed and hugged her daughter, and they walked arm in arm back to the arena. They watched Mandy for a while, then Colonel Paul came over and said yes, that Anne could get and tack Checkers by herself if Kate could supervise.

"I've got to check on one of the mares up there," he said gesturing over beyond the arena. "She's stocked up in the hind legs, and I like to massage and rewrap them every couple hours, trying to get the fluid to move out."

Half an hour later, Colonel Paul joined Kate watching Anne walk around in the ring. Mandy had taken Noble to the barn to untack and turn him back out in his pasture. Rather than agonize over this courage he didn't seem to have, he just said: "Would you like to ride,

Kate? Big Dan has cut trails nearly to the top of that hill through the woods, and we can walk across the top of the property and down the other side. Just a walk," he assured her when she said it had been years since she'd ridden. "I'm just getting back into the saddle myself. You can ride Noble, and I'll take Cash. Tomorrow, 3:30? It's always a break time for me."

Kate gulped, wondering if she could make the drive again. Anne wouldn't be here, and it wasn't one of Mandy's work days. "Okay," she said. "But if I can't come …"

"If you can't come, here, call my cell phone. I'm here every day, so you can let me know what's best," he suggested.

Kate felt like a fool, already setting up an alternative if she couldn't drive here by herself tomorrow. She determined that she'd think positive, and how she would love to ride again. She asked the ladies Bible study group that night at her house to pray for her specifically for the drive at 3:15 the next afternoon. They'd been praying for her since she began hosting the meetings, and she was experiencing answers and strength.

The next day, she pulled into Amethyst Valley at 3:20, feeling calm and quite proud of herself. Now she was more apprehensive about riding a horse again than the drive! She found Colonel Paul in the barn, with both horses tacked and tied nearby. Two riders were practicing in the arena, and they waited until they could ride in there to warm up.

"Noble is very calm. He doesn't spook or get excited about anything, so you'll be fine. There's nothing shameful about holding onto the horn the entire time. He is a direct rein horse from his training, but he'll neck rein, and mostly, he'll follow, so you don't have to do much. I've taken Cash out on the trails a few times. He's nervous, not in a high strung way, but he spooks easily if he steps on a twig or something rustles in the bushes, like a rabbit one day. I like him a lot. He's strong and solid and real sure-footed. Don't worry, Noble won't spook, even if Cash does."

They chatted about the farm and other horses. He pointed to them one by one and told her their names, ages, breeds, personalities, while they waited for the arena to clear. Finally, Mrs. White and the other rider dismounted and returned to the barn.

Kate walked Noble to the mounting block, tightened his cinch and took a deep breath. She carefully stood up, put her left foot into the stirrup and lightly swung up and over, seating herself gently and flawlessly in the saddle. She got settled, and urged Noble to walk forward from the mounting block.

Colonel Paul turned Cash around to the other side. He now mounted from a horse's right side, so he didn't put all his weight on the lower left leg and artificial foot. He wasn't sure how to get the feel of his left foot being in the stirrup and keep it there. Big Dan solved that problem by imbedding a substantial magnet into the bottom on his left cowboy boot. He affixed the attracting magnet to the stirrup, so the Colonel could hear the click and feel the security when the magnets met. Then he could put enough pressure down to keep the boot in the stirrup. In an emergency, the magnetism wouldn't be strong enough to hold, and his foot would come right out.

They walked around the arena for 15 minutes, and then walked out, around it and started up the trail. It was easy walking. Dan had cleared a good four to five feet wide, even grinding out some tree stumps so there was nothing for the horses to trip or step on that might inhibit their footing. Still, it wasn't enough to ride side by side, and there were some narrow turns.

Colonel Paul liked riding up here every day, partly for Cash's training and partly to pack down the trail. Most of the boarders seemed content riding in the arena, except Mrs. White. She was the first one up the trails, going as far as she could, then turning around and riding back down, and up and down again, even when it was just 30 feet. She so loved being on Harmony.

Given Noble's super calm personality, Colonel Paul figured he would not care where he was in a trail ride line up - leading, following or being last. His suspicion about Cash was confirmed that day when they tried riding side by side walking from the arena to the trail. Cash cared very much that he was first, so he kept speeding up so he'd always be ahead of Noble. Kate was thrilled with every step. Noble was the tallest horse she'd ever ridden, and she was instantly comfortable with him. Of course, she had met him a couple times and heard so much about him. She knew he was very calm, and she also called on her "Noble Spirit" when she needed to be strong, usually driving alone.

This day, Kate figured when they were at the bottom, she'd be okay near the house and barn, and when they were at the top, she'd be somewhat near her house, down the other side. What took her by surprise was once they got into the woods, about a third of the way up, her heart started pounding. Her hands got sweaty, and she felt closed in and panicky. She couldn't see anything but dense trees and the trail. She was terrified.

"Can we turn around now?" she said loudly to Colonel Paul. He heard the edge in her voice. He sensed anxiety.

"Indeed, Kate. I'm turning right now. You want to turn and head down first?"

"No," she said, try to speak smoothly though her heart was gripped with fear. "You go first."

He passed her and walked back down. As the trail came to an end, and she saw the barn and her car, she felt a little better. They walked to the edge of the arena and dismounted.

"I can take the horses from here, if you want to go home," he said.

Kate struggled inside. She wanted to stay and untack and brush Noble and help. But she wanted so much to go home, too. Still trying to steady her voice, she said, "I want to stay, but I need to go home now."

"Okay, hey, Kate, it's okay. We'll do it again."

She went to her car, tears streaming down her cheeks that no one could see. She turned right on State Highway 24 and gunned it a little too much in her hurry to get home. She traveled as far as she dared when she heard the siren and saw the flashing lights in her rearview mirror, knowing she'd be less anxious the closer she got to the grocery store and something familiar.

A Noble Spirit

Chapter
15

"Where's the fire, miss?" asked the officer in her driver window. He saw she was upset, but she was speeding, and he was doing his job.

"No fire, sir, just a little nervous and in a hurry to get home, sorry," Kate said, reaching into her purse for her license. She handed it to him and fumbled in the glove compartment for the registration.

"Never mind, Mrs. Dawson," the policeman said abruptly, "I'm just giving you a verbal warning this time, and, if it's okay with you, I'll escort you over to 344 Newport Street. Don't lose me going too fast, okay?" He handed her back her license.

"Thank you, thank you, officer Cole," Kate said, noting his shiny name tag. She waited until he was back in the patrol car before putting the Mercury into gear and driving back on the highway and slowly and safely home. He continued on when she turned into her driveway. Kate walked into the house and went straight to her bedroom, closing the door and falling, sobbing, on her bed. She was so embarrassed and so ashamed of her behavior and her fear.

Why? Why did she have this agoraphobia? Where did it come from? She remembered the days late in her marriage when she'd go nuts in a movie theatre or at the dentist or tried to drive once to a Kohl's store only a couple miles away. She knew one thing. Because of it, she was very sensitive to others and their struggles with weight or alcohol or drugs or eating. She refused to take any tranquilizers or medicines that would dull her awareness or create side effects.

And she knew something else. She would not give up. For Anne. For herself. For her sanity and sense of self-worth. She would go back to the horse farm. She would ride again. She would go a little farther every time. How she would explain any of this to that nice looking Colonel, she had no idea. Certainly, he would think she was a fool. That's okay. The last thing she needed was a romantic interest anyway. She had a daughter to raise, a living to make, a life to live, a condition that baffled her to overcome. And she could go to the grocery store now and to Martha's house and to the horse farm. She got up and went to make dinner.

The next Wednesday night at Bible study, Kate shared her experience. "The officer was so nice …" she stopped mid-sentence and looked across the room at Rebecca Cole. "Is he …?"

"One and the same," she chirped. "He's my husband, and I asked him to help you if he ever saw you around town. I told him what kind of car you drive and what color, but he didn't remember until he saw your driver's license."

Kate got up early the next morning to do her medical billing work so she could drive to Amethyst Valley Horse Farm again. Anne offered to ride with her, and they could pick up Mandy, but Kate refused.

"You go over the big hill, honey, with Mandy. I need to do this by myself," she explained.

"Okay," said Anne. "I'll be watching for you! And, I know you can do it again!"

And she did. Kate got more and more comfortable with the drive, going days when Mandy and Anne were there. Colonel Paul said they could ride when she was ready, which was just a few days later.

This time, she made it to the top and across the pasture. They stopped at the hilltop hideout, and he told her about seeing the matted grass and a girl trying to hide behind an apple tree trunk the day he was fixing fences. It was Mandy. He explained about watching her and Anne up here with Noble.

"I knew he was a pretty safe horse. We can't bubble wrap kids like some are trying to do. I loved that they weren't inside watching TV or playing computer games, so I kept an eye out almost every afternoon. They're good girls. They were even up here in the rain a couple times."

Natalie suggested to Colonel Paul that he ride the 200 or so acres on the other side to see what was suitable for trails, pastures or hay. Kate went with him a few times, and only once did she ask to turn back.

He wasn't a talking kind of man, and she grew to feel safe with him. Little by little, astride Noble and Cash, they walked the new trails both ways, checked fences and surveyed the farm from all angles. Soon the Army man and the emotionally insecure, single mom were sharing stories of travels and trials, challenges and victories, love and loss, families and foibles. She had heard from Anne and Mandy of his incredible patience and kindness with the horses. "He's firm and makes them do what he wants," Anne had explained recently, "but you can tell he loves them all and communicates with a gentle voice and body language. He's brilliant with horses, and they walk to him whenever they see him coming. Except Cash. He doesn't walk to anyone, but at least he stands still instead of walking away now."

He told her about his childhood and how the horses gave him confidence, while he liked to think he gave the same to them. He slowly opened up about his Army experiences, working with the horses at Fort Bragg, his tours of duty, the explosion, his next memory waking up in a military hospital in Germany and the rehab at the VA hospital. "I could have stayed in the Army, I suppose, but I guess it seemed like time to find a life of my own."

For her part, she talked about her wonderful childhood, her parents, her father's death when she was 16 and then the unexpected – and unwanted – anxiety and panic attacks. "The average age they begin is 20," she explained. "I don't have anything traumatic that happened, like some people do, but all the same, I get terribly frightened for no reason. It's so frustrating." She didn't add how inferior it made her feel.

He listened intently, always stopping and turning his attention on what she was saying, even though he didn't always respond. He was acutely aware of the psychological screening the Army undertook to qualify a soldier for special operations, and fear and anxiety issues were high on the list. He silently wondered if losing her father and having a baby in a two-year span could have triggered the condition.

One day she stopped and turned to him. "I think you have a 'Noble Spirit,' just like this Thoroughbred," she said, stroking the big horse's withers in front of the saddle. "Strong, calm, quiet and ... and ... noble." She flushed a little at the sound of her own voice speaking that way. He knew about the Noble Spirit Horse Club, and she had told him about Mandy's and Anne's "Noble Spirit."

Colonel Paul smiled. He didn't know what to say, so he didn't say anything. As they walked along across the high pasture, Kate thought about how comfortable silence was with Colonel Paul. She never felt the need to begin conversation once it naturally came to an end of a topic or observation. Sometimes they talked a lot, sharing experiences and their views on a wide range of life issues. But usually there were quiet times in between talking times, and she grew to like the spaces. They even talked about this once.

"I'm a slow thinker," Colonel Paul had said. "So I like to mull over in my mind what someone has just said or explained or shared. I don't understand people as well as horses, so I take my time and ponder their words and behavior. Do you know," he said in a brighter tone, "that people's body language often contradicts what they say?"

When Kate said she wasn't sure she understood, he explained. "Here's one example: The other day on television, there was an all-messed up family on 'Dr. Phil,' and he was asking the father a question. The father responded saying that such-and-such wasn't a big deal at all, but his hands were wide apart, which expresses something large. So he's saying it's not important, but his arms spread wide tell a different story. Haven't you ever seen someone saying yes while shaking their head, even slightly, side to side in a negative way?"

When she said she had not noticed, he explained a few more ways people say something with their body movements and contradict it with their words. She asked if he learned this in the Army, if it was part of his training, and he said no. He told her he'd been noticing this stuff since he was a little boy. "Except for my grandmother, I don't think I knew anyone who was truthful with words until I got into the Army. My grandma was a great, strong, quiet woman who said a person could be measured most accurately by actions and deeds and faith, not words. She was the most loving and perceptive person I have ever known." His voice trailed off, and Kate felt another quiet time had arrived. They moved off at a slow walk.

Back at the barn, they unsaddled, brushed the horses and walked them back to their pasture. Kate told him about the new horse club, and they talked about things the girls could do. Colonel Paul offered to have club members come to the farm, and he would show them the basics of horse anatomy and horse care. He suggested they could come when one of the farriers would be shoeing and trimming horses, too.

Just before falling asleep, Colonel Paul thought about Kate. He hadn't seen any contradiction in her words and body language. He looked forward to their rides and time together, and with ever so small a smile, he fell asleep. For a few hours.

Colonel Paul opened his eyes, looked at the clock and instinctively reached for his loaded sidearm which rested in a holster he'd mounted to the back of the nightstand. 2:10 a.m. The crunch on gravel ceased, and he guessed that a vehicle stopped on the opposite side of the barn from his cabin. A car door opened, maybe two. He did not hear them close.

Thankful for weeks of practice to increase speed at installing his prosthetic foot device, he was standing with black pants and low rise Muck® boots on in less than two minutes. He pulled on the black shirt he left on the bed post every night and noiselessly crossed the living room to his front door.

Chapter
16

Staying in the shadows of the barn wall on this half moon, clear night, Colonel Paul heard two horses nicker in the barn. He walked to the back sliding door which was open about a foot. Someone stood at Apache's stall door, and a second person was opening it.

"Who goes there?" asked Colonel Paul quietly, slipping sideways through the door and intentionally shining his flashlight at the barn floor so the horses would not be startled. However, with the stall door partly opened by now, Apache did spook, pushing his way through the open door. The person in the way fell sideways, and the door struck the other one. Both were knocked to the floor with muffled screams, and the horse ran right for Colonel Paul.

"Easy boy, e-e-e-easy boy, it's okay, e-e-e-easy big boy," Colonel Paul said in a low, calm voice. The big horse halted about a foot from him and the door, eyes blazing, head high, frightened, but listening to the reassuring voice that all the horses knew. The man reached for a lead rope on the closest stall door and placed it slowly and gently around the Warmblood's neck. He stroked his shoulder and neck, encouraging Apache to lower his head, thus relaxing from his fright. The two people had gotten up.

"It's Rachel. I'm so sorry, Colonel Paul." She was crying. "I lost my cell phone somewhere, and my boyfriend and I came to check Apache's stall. I haven't had it since I was here this afternoon. Maybe I dropped it when I put him back," said the 18-year-old owner of the spirited horse.

Colonel Paul turned on some lights and walked the now calm horse back to his stall, checking his muzzle, legs and body for any injury. He figured the horse simply pushed the stall door with his nose or chest, and there were no noticeable marks. He'd check again in the morning for swelling or tenderness. Rachel and her boyfriend – a young man Colonel Paul had seen a few times watching her ride – had dusted themselves off and appeared unhurt.

He turned on the light in the tack room and moved a couple chairs. "Come and sit down," he said, sliding the safety back on the concealed hand gun and keeping it out of sight. He reached into the small refrigerator, took out three bottles of water, unscrewed the caps and handed one to each of them.

Colonel Paul had a reputation of being very perceptive. It seemed like he could see everywhere at once. He knew what was going on with every horse and every person on the farm every day. He was also always honest and expected the same from everyone. He looked from one to the other. Rachel told him about being at a party where things got out of control. There was some drinking. A couple guys got into a bad fight, and the police were called. Rachel and her boyfriend left a few minutes before the ambulance and cops got there.

"My parents warned me about those kids," she said, beginning to cry again, "but I wouldn't listen. I thought it would be cool to hang out with a fast crowd. But it's not cool. When I got scared, they made fun of me and said I wasn't very grown up for my age. But I don't think fighting and drinking are very grown up, do you, Colonel Paul?"

"No, Rachel, I do not. You were smart – and grown up – to leave. Both of you," he said gesturing to the young man. Rachel introduced him as her boyfriend, Andy. She had told her parents she was sleeping over at a girl friend's house, even though they didn't like her friendship with this girl. She was 18, after all, and they asked that she check in with them by noon the next day. "My parents were right about these kids and that girl. They're jerks. And now, it's too late to go home, and I don't know what to do or where to go, and I need to find my cell phone."

Colonel Paul handed her the phone he found in the stall when he put Apache back. "Go home now, Rachel. If your parents wake up, tell them the truth. If not, tell them in the morning. Are you okay to go home, son?" he asked Andy.

"Sure, it doesn't much matter what I do. My dad doesn't care if I come or go or whatever," he responded, hanging his head sadly. Rachel reached for his hand, and he perked up. "Rachel has given me a reason to finish high school and think about the future and my purpose in life. I had an aunt and grandmother who cared for me, but they died. I never had a mother."

Colonel Paul knew those feelings of being alone in the world at such a tender age. He turned to horses. Andy had found a nice girlfriend. "If you want to come back after taking Rachel home, you can crash this once at my cabin," he offered.

"Okay, thanks," said Andy, rising from his chair. They left, and Colonel Paul checked all the stall doors. He patted a couple horse foreheads before ascending the ladder at one end of the tack room. He stepped down the ladder rungs carrying one U.S. Army issue olive green cot, a sleeping bag and pillow, all neatly packed in a canvas bag. He headed back to the cabin to prepare for his guest.

The Noble Spirit Horse Club had its first meeting the second Tuesday afternoon in July with seven members: Mandy, Anne, Rachel and Mrs. White from the farm, two girls from church and a girl named Razia who read it in the grocery store. She had her own horse at home and went to a boarding school during the year. They decided right away that Kate was also a member, then Mrs. White wouldn't feel funny being the only adult. So that made eight.

Kate brought the meeting to order and explained Robert's Rules of Order and how things are organized in a club and a meeting. Mrs. White volunteered to be the secretary and take minutes. They didn't need a treasurer. The girls asked Mandy to be the president and

Anne the vice president since it was their idea and, except for Razia, they had the most exposure to real horses.

Since everything was "new business," they started with the idea of splitting the meetings into three categories, which would all be "old business" the next week: (1) each one or some of them could share something she learned about horses since the previous meeting or a horse book she was reading; (2) they would talk of community things they could do as a club, volunteering or being in next year's parade, even if they walked, maybe with a banner; (3) Mandy had spoken to Mrs. Adams about having a small horse show.

They decided to wait one week on the first item, so they could come prepared. The girls definitely wanted to do something in next year's 4th of July parade, but that was a long ways off. Then Mandy brought up the horse show at the end of the summer.

"I talked to Mrs. Adams and Colonel Paul about the new club and if they had any ideas what we could do. They said if we organize a small horse show, we can have it at Amethyst Valley. Mrs. Adams will rent bleachers and a big tent for what she called a chuckwagon picnic. She'll have barbecue, buns, beans, cole slaw, lemonade and iced tea, and everyone coming can bring a potluck dish. I'm sure it will be very small this first time, but it could become something we do every year on Labor Day, the day before school starts."

The room buzzed with excitement, and Mrs. White scribbled as fast as she could when Kate rattled off more than a dozen show ideas, explaining each one. "With egg and spoon, you give everyone on horseback a plastic spoon and one real egg. They hold the egg in the spoon with one hand and walk around, change direction, trot and walk as the announcer instructs. The eggs fall off easily, so the winner is the last one still holding an egg in spoon." She told them about ride-a-buck, go as you please and halter classes, potato runs and the slow race. "In the slow race, the horses have to move forward all the time, and the last one to cross the finish line wins. But they can't stop. It's hard to get a horse to walk super slow."

"Oh, I almost forgot," said Mandy. "Mrs. Adams also said she'll buy some ribbons for awards. She said it's not a real horse show without ribbons. She's so nice. She said she'll have papers for everyone to sign. She's a lawyer, you know, and she wants to come next week to talk to us."

Kate remembered more events from her horse camp experiences, and they talked about everything from entry fees to age groups and how to make and where to distribute flyers. They decided to start small and just put information on public bulletin boards around town. They settled on 20 classes, five for children 12 and under, five for ages 13-19, and 10 for everyone, including the youngsters. No dress rules or anything fancy. They could eliminate classes for which no one signed up. They wanted anyone with a pony or horse to come for fun and hoped others would attend as spectators and for the picnic. They would charge $3 entry to the show per family, and one dollar to enter each class.

When Mandy told Mrs. Adams about the charges, she suggested that the club keep the money to pay for printing flyers and whatever they might need. At the next meeting, one of the girls from church became the treasurer, with Kate's help.

News traveled fast, and the following week at the mall, Mandy saw the Wicked Three. Oh, no, she thought. Not them.

"Hey, Mandy," Jennifer called as all three approached. Mandy figured she had not grown any taller, and she hoped they'd run out of tall jokes and digs.

Amanda spoke first. "We heard about the horse club and the show. We don't have horses, but I love them. If I could join or help, well, I'd like to be friends."

"And us, too," chimed in Kerry and Jennifer. "Is there anything we can do, or, um, can we join?"

Of course, Mandy wanted to say, yes, that there was something they could do. They could all get lost! She was instantly reminded of Pastor Porter's sermon two weeks ago about kindness and how you can only control your own actions, not the actions of others. He spoke about finding something good in everyone. She also thought of her "Noble Spirit" – that strength and calm she could use when she was feeling challenged.

"Well, let me think," Mandy said, remembering the club's eight members and the long list of things to do. Jennifer had the voice of a crystal clear bird, if there were such a bird. She could sing the national anthem. She knew that Amanda had a keyboard and had taken some lessons. Kerry had the lead two years in a row in the school play. She was a strong, clear speaker, with or without a microphone.

"Well, I'll have to talk to the other club members about your joining. I mean, you haven't been really friendly and all, and this is a special club where we all respect one another and work together," Mandy said, hoping she didn't sound too unfriendly. These girls had not been nice to her for a long time. She loved the new Noble Spirit Horse Club, and she wanted to be sure everyone would get along and work as a team on community activities and the horse show.

"We are going to do some volunteer work as a group," she continued, "and everyone will have responsibilities for organizing and working at the horse show. The club wants to help others, share things we learn about horses and, well, just be horse friends as one group with no small groups that are separate."

"We will," they said in unison.

"Mandy, I will be nice to everyone, really I will," Jennifer said with a sort of sorry and sincere look.

"Okay, we meet on Tuesday afternoons. I'll call you after the meeting. I just feel like I should check with everyone," Mandy explained.

The Wicked Three didn't look so wicked now. They were all smiles, and one by one they gave Mandy a hug and thanked her for talking to the current horse club members and hoping they could join.

Rachel came to the club meeting the next week. Kate explained again how Robert's Rules of Order worked, and after Mrs. White's minutes were approved, Anne told about learning about the frog on the bottom of a horse's foot.

"I don't know why they call it a frog, but I drew a picture. It's like a V, and you want to pick out dirt and little stones or stuff so it doesn't get infected or cause thrush – it's like an infection and can travel up the hoof and take a long time to heal," she explained.

Razia brought photos of her horse, Desert Sunshine or "Sunny," and talked about Arabians, which is the oldest known breed of riding horse. They are prized for beauty, intelligence and endurance. Napoleon, Alexander the Great and George Washington rode Arabians. She pointed out Sunny's distinctive characteristics like a dished profile, large, wide-set eyes, small ears, a broad forehead and large nostrils. She also told the group that her mother is American, and her father is from Saudi Arabia, and they have two Arabians and one Arabian-Thoroughbred horse.

A few other girls shared horse-related things. Mrs. White brought photos, too, and planned to talk about cribbing, but she noted the time and saved it for another meeting. Mandy told the group about Jennifer, Kerry and Amanda wanting to join the club.

"Do you want them?" asked Anne. "They're always so not nice to you!"

"I know," Mandy replied. "But our only requirement is that members love horses, and they said they all love horses, and that they'll be nice and work together. I say we give them a chance to be in the club, and if they become a clique of their own, well, Mrs. Dawson, can you talk to them if it happens?"

Kate agreed to pay attention to them while hoping they joined in with everyone. Mandy called Jennifer that night and the following Tuesday, the Wicked Three showed up, and the group now had 12 members. Natalie Adams was there, too, and what she had to say under "new business" thrilled everyone.

"I'm going to be home all day this Saturday, and I'm taking off the first week of August," she began. "I know most of you do not have horses of your own or a lot of horse experience, but there are some horses at the farm you can learn to lead, stop, turn and walk over obstacles. If you want to plan a day, I'll be there and show you some of my horses which are very well trained. Rachel said we can use her pony, Checkers, too, and Colonel Paul has Noble available. Maybe we can match up each one who doesn't have a horse with a horse and a class or two, so everyone can be a participant in your Noble Spirit Horse Club Show at Amethyst Valley."

She said that everyone needed to sign a waiver, wear boots with heels, no sneakers or smooth sole shoes, and a helmet. "I have three helmets which can be borrowed, and some of you may wish to buy your own."

The girls were ecstatic. Natalie and Kate planned to get together soon to go over all the classes and ideas and finalize a list of horse show events in which everyone could enter at least two classes. As the meeting was coming to a close, a car turned into Kate's driveway, then everyone heard acceleration and a crash!

A Noble Spirit

Chapter
17

Kate grabbed her cell phone and dialed 9-1-1 on the way out the door. The girls were at her heels, except Jennifer, who was simply looking out the window. A metallic red Jaguar had driven right into Kate's small station wagon. The air bag was inflated, and a woman was fighting and screaming that she couldn't breathe and to get her out!

Kate calmly spoke to her and carefully moved the air bag, which was already starting to deflate, over to the passenger side so the driver could see and breathe. Before Kate would let the woman get out of the car, she kneeled down next to her, checking for any injuries which might be complicated by her moving and getting out of the car.

"Leave me alone. Get out of here," the woman screeched, maneuvering her way out of the car and standing next to it, smoothing her dress and trying to wipe her face. Then she started laughing and pointing to the cars."

"Mrs. Gardner, are you okay?" asked Amanda, trying to hold

the woman's arm and steady her. Just then, a police car arrived, the ambulance pulled in and paramedics approached the angry woman. She slapped at one of them, and Kate suggested they all just stand there and catch their breath. A few other moms and a dad arrived to pick up the others, and Kate told Anne and Mandy to go back into the house. Mrs. White left.

The folks outside convinced Mrs. Gardner, Jennifer's mother, to get into the ambulance and go to the hospital for a thorough examination following her ordeal. Natalie departed in her Explorer, and Kate returned to the house, where Anne, Jennifer and Mandy were in the living room. "Well," said Jennifer flatly, "now you all sort of met my drunk mother. I hate her. And if you go to the hospital, you can meet my workaholic, ER doctor father. I hate him, too."

Kate put her arm around Jennifer, who pulled away. "We never know what struggles are going on inside a person," she said gently. She should know. "Be patient, Jennifer, and maybe we can figure a way to help."

"Let's go to the hilltop hideout, Jennifer," Mandy suggested, remembering that Anne had an extra art lesson late that afternoon. "I'll show you where we watch the horse farm and then walk to my house." Jennifer got her papers and backpack and nodded affirmative. They walked in silence. Mandy showed her where she first saw Noble and told her about riding him up there bareback. She pointed out the various horses and their breeds and names. They saw Colonel Paul working with Cash. Jennifer said nothing.

When they got to Mandy's house, it was close to 5:30. Her mother knew about the incident from Kate already and simply welcomed Jennifer to their home. Indeed, she was beautiful, Martha thought, remembering Danny's observations. She said that Dr. Gardner had called and would pick her up in 45 minutes. Jennifer said nothing. Danny made a cheerful appearance, surprised to see Jennifer, but he was cool and asked about the club meeting and horse show planning. Jennifer was so upset, she didn't even try to impress this boy she had a crush on. She said nothing.

"I'm going to be in charge of traffic," he told Jennifer while acting quite important. "So, me and the guys, we get to stand in the road legally and stop cars and direct trucks and horse trailers. It's gonna be neat." He sensed something amiss, so he wandered off to his room. Jennifer said nothing.

Big Dan walked in the front door just a few minutes before Dr. Gardner arrived, with Mrs. Gardner in the car. He came inside, and Jennifer finally spoke. "I don't want to go home with you. I don't want to go home at all." The doctor appeared immensely distressed in this situation.

Big Dan stepped in. "We are going for pizza in a little while. Why don't you go home, regroup, freshen up, and meet us at Fran's Pizza Parlor in, say, an hour?"

"Can we?" Jennifer asked her father.

He hesitated, looked toward the car, then responded: "Okay, if you want to. We can do that."

With that, Jennifer got into the back seat of the late model, white Lexus, slammed the door, and they pulled out of the driveway.

"Pizza?" Martha queried.

"Well, someone had to say something, and it was the first thing that came to my mind. From what you told me briefly, it sounds like the family needs help, and pizza is a good place to start," Mandy's dad stated. Of course, he wondered if the doctor's family ever ate pizza. They lived in a veritable mansion outside of town. Mandy didn't know where they lived. She was just glad, at that moment, that she didn't live there.

An hour later, Dr. Gardner and Jennifer walked into the pizza place. They had saved three places, and quickly rearranged things for two. A couple of Danny's friends showed up and dragged up a couple more chairs. The teenagers gravitated to one end of the long table as four different pizzas were passed around and sodas were re-filled.

The doctor joined Big Dan with a Heineken, and the three adults chatted amicably about construction work, the real estate market, jobs, healthcare issues that were making the news and the weather. People always talk about the weather somewhere along the way. Martha asked about Mrs. Gardner, who apparently was more embarrassed and shaken up than injured. The doctor said she simply didn't want to see anyone, and her face was already beginning to show bruising from the airbag.

Out of the blue, Martha piped up, "There's a men's retreat with our church, Amethyst Valley Bible Church, in two weeks. You'd be welcome to go, Dr. Gardner."

"Call me Sam, please," said the physician. "Oh, golly, I don't know. I usually work on weekends. It's the busiest time in the ER, as you can imagine."

"Well, you mentioned that there are four other doctors rotating. It's not like one person can work 24/7," Dan said. "We don't bring any beer, of course, and we don't hold hands and sing, like the women (he winked at Martha). It's just a guy time of sharing and talking and hearing about how God planned for us to live. We go Friday about 5 p.m. for 24 hours. It's good, Sam, it's a good time to look at things. Some talk about stuff, some don't, but we can trust one another. Sort of that old saw, what is brought up at the men's retreat, stays at the men's retreat. You could ride with me in my pick-up truck." He instantly wished he hadn't said that. Sam had probably never been in a pick-up truck.

"I'll think about it," he responded. "Here I am. An ER doctor who evaluates people every day and quickly ascertains a plan of action and moves forward confidently, saving lives and limbs. My home, however, is ... well, we have our challenges." He took a deep breath and sighed. "I don't know what to do about it."

Jennifer didn't hear any of this, but at this moment, she got up and approached. "Dad, the kids are all going to the drive-in movies. Can I go with them and sleep over at Mandy's house?" Mandy smiled to her mom.

Sam sat for a minute looking at his beautiful daughter. "Sure, Jen, you go and have a good time, if it's okay with Mandy's parents (who were nodding approval). Let me give you enough money for the ticket, and buy popcorn for everyone." He handed her $50. She stopped, like she wanted to hug him or something, but she did not. "Okay, Dad," was all she said.

The doctor pulled out his wallet again when the pizza bill came, but Big Dan picked it up first. "If I knew you were buying, we would've gone to the Silk Room Inn," he quipped. "The pizza is on me, no argument."

A week later, Sam called Big Dan and said he got the weekend off to go to the men's retreat, and he would take him up on the pick-up truck ride, too.

That Saturday, all the horse club girls were at the farm planning for the horse show and meeting Natalie's horses, so Martha decided to visit Mrs. Gardner. Early in the day. Just in case. She called first to be sure she would be at home.

Martha found the house easily with Big Dan's directions. It would be impossible to miss the three-story, contemporary glass and cedar house snuggled into a hillside near the top of the West Garrison Road, a back way to the next county. Mrs. Gardner met her in the driveway and seemed so pleased to have a visitor. They had coffee on a deck overlooking two more decks and a swimming pool and talked about the girls and the horse club. Martha asked about her childhood and how she and doctor met.

Mrs. Gardner – "please call me Carol" – was a charming lady raised in Barcelona, Spain, where her father worked for an international company. She had a bachelor's degree in fine arts and hoped one day to own a gallery where she could showcase regional artists and fine crafts, as well as her own watercolors and jewelry. She and Sam met on an art appreciation trip in France.

"The house was Sam's idea," she said. "I think it's a shrine to his success as a doctor, even though he's not here very much. And we had a reason we wanted to move from our old house. He didn't want me to go to work. He thought it would look like he didn't make enough money. Did you know he is also the head physician for the university football team an hour away – that takes up all Fall weekends – and he serves on the board of directors at the bank, the big car dealership and that company, whatever-it's-called, down on State Highway 24? He's busy all the time. Jennifer won't let me into her life at all. I just take her to voice lessons, the mall and Amanda and Kerry's houses. They are inseparable, those three, and she sleeps over with them almost every weekend."

Martha poured more coffee for both of them. "I get so lonely way up here," she said. "The car accident at Kate's was a real wake-up call, not to mention embarrassment for Sam and Jennifer. I feel like they are ashamed of me, and honestly, Martha, I'm ashamed of myself. I used to volunteer and paint, but I lost interest. My family still lives in Spain, and Sam's folks are in Oregon. I feel sometimes like I cannot be me. I need to function as the doctor's wife. I don't know where I fit in any more."

By the time Mandy and Jennifer called for a ride, it was nearly 2 p.m. "More than anything, I need to do something to feel productive and useful. I'm not an alcoholic," Carol said. "I really want so much to live in town and have neighbors. All this," she waved her arms around, "may spell success, but not if you don't love it, or like Sam, if you're not here enough to enjoy it, what's the point?"

Her face lit up when she talked about art and art galleries. She showed Martha some of her paintings, and Martha was awestruck with the detail, especially in the fabric, since that was her area of expertise. "You capture those blue jeans and the folds in that jacket so perfectly. It looks like I can touch it and actually feel the texture."

Martha attended a couple bridal fairs each year to stay up on trends and fabrics, and Carol agreed to go with her in the fall and visit art galleries in the city. They also decided to go to lunch the following week with their daughters. Before she got into her car, Martha stood in the driveway, held Carol's hand and prayed for their new friendship, a renewed interest and energy in her art and more communication and time together for her, Sam and Jennifer as a family.

Of course, she invited her to the every-other-Wednesday night ladies Bible study group at Kate's house. "Are you sure they'd want me?" Carol asked. "I don't know if my car will be fixed by then, and I think I'll be quite embarrassed to see Kate. I don't know much about the Bible either." Martha convinced her quickly that every woman in the Bible study had done something stupid, and if she wanted to compare notes, well, "there are events that top that car crash," she added with a knowing smile. "I'll pick you up."

The day at the horse farm was informative and fun for everyone in the club. Razia had prior plans, but all the other girls, Kate and Mrs. White were there. Natalie always looked so corporate, but this day she looked like a professional horsewoman in black riding pants and paddock boots and a white tee shirt with an embroidered brown horse on it. She went over basic horse safety and categorized everyone according to experience. Jennifer, Amanda and Kerry were the only ones who had never been near or on a horse.

Mrs. Adams pointed out her horses, and decided that day to

use Noble, Paloosa, Checkers and Viking to teach leading, turning, stopping and a quick release knot. She suggested Mandy and Mrs. White supervise letting each girl lead a horse around the arena, tie it up, untie and lead around again. Then, each girl could mount and dismount, if all went well, they could walk in the arena. She went to the house to make a phone call. As she turned to leave, Jennifer walked over to her.

"Mrs. Adams," she began, "that white horse, can I learn to lead her and ride her? She's gorgeous, and I'll do everything exactly as you tell me. These horses are really cool, but she ... she ... she is like out of a fairy tale." Natalie smiled. Kazi had taken lots of blue ribbons under saddle and in lead, but she could have her own agenda, too. She promised Jennifer that maybe next time she'd bring Kazi to the ring.

"You learn today to lead, tie, mount and dismount, and we'll talk about Kazi next week," she said. Jennifer lead both Noble and Paloosa around as she was instructed, tied the slipknot perfectly each time and mounted and dismounted comfortably. She even walked mounted by herself a couple times. But, all the while, she could hardly take her eyes off Kazi.

Martha left Carol's house to pick up the girls and pulled into the horse farm right behind an old pick up marked Perez Brothers Fencing. Mandy and Jennifer were visiting a white horse in the back pasture. Colonel Paul was leaving the round pen when a stout, dark-haired man jumped out of the truck and frantically approached him. He held Colonel Paul's arm and spoke rapidly in Spanish. Martha sensed desperation in his voice and stood quietly by her car waiting for the girls.

A Noble Spirit

Chapter
18

After a few minutes of conversation, Colonel Paul asked Martha to wait there, and he went to the big house. When he returned, he took Martha aside and asked if Mandy could come along on an important mission. He explained that Manuel Perez' 5-year-old granddaughter had been missing for several hours in the woods behind where the family lived.

"Apparently, there are some immigration legal issues, and Manuel does not dare go to the police," he explained. "He said the little girl had been warned about strange men, and he doesn't think she'll come to me. He says there are forest roads over there, and I'd like to take Mandy and Noble with me. I'm going to use one of Natalie's horse trailers."

Martha trusted Colonel Paul and knew he wouldn't ask if he didn't also trust Mandy and think she could help. "Okay. I need to take Jennifer home, and I'll call Dan. He knows his way all around the county."

So it was that Martha took Jennifer home with minimal explanation, while Mandy got Noble saddled and gathered his and Cash's bridles. Colonel Paul retrieved Cash from the round pen, stopping first at his cabin for a few supplies and a second shirt. He tied a blue cantle bag with supplies and a small blanket on the back of his saddle.

In the meantime, Manuel had lined up one of Natalie's trucks with a horse trailer. Colonel Paul hooked it up with ease, then loaded Cash and Noble. Mandy jumped into the front seat, and Colonel Paul gave her the details while he followed Manuel's truck. They went about seven miles along State Highway 24 before turning at a rusty mailbox with the number 3488 barely visible. They passed one small farm, and two miles farther, they came to an old house and two trailers, more like campers.

Big Dan called Colonel Paul's cell phone, and they exchanged information and directions with the promise that he and Danny would show up as fast as they could get there and search on foot. By the time the horses were unloaded, cinches tightened and bridles placed on over the halters with their lead ropes tied on the saddle horns, Mandy's dad and brother pulled up.

"I know this area well," said Big Dan, pulling out a topographical map and a county road map. He pointed out the forest roads and trails, noting that there was a campground on the other side of the big hill, about two miles away. He suggested that Colonel Paul and Mandy take the horses that way, while he and Danny would walk in a circle to the east of that.

"Most likely a little girl is going to stay on a path, not bushwhack through some dense brush, unless something scares her," he commented. Manuel came over with a couple men and two women to go on the walking search. He showed them on the map where they last saw her playing with a jar of bubbles. He spoke enough English to understand everything, and they headed out.

Mandy's heart was pounding at first, and in this situation, she drew on her "Noble Spirit" in a different way. She looked at the sky and silently asked for strength and alertness for her and for God's direction and guidance in rescuing the little girl, Marina.

"Are you okay?" asked Colonel Paul.

"Yes," responded Mandy, taking a deep breath.

Chapter 18

He was taking a chance with her being young and not an experienced rider, but he needed a female along, since Manuel said Marina was somewhat frightened of strangers, especially men. Time was of the essence, or he might have called Kate, and he trusted Noble, the ever calm, willing Thoroughbred.

They rode in silence at a slow walk for more than 30 minutes, Noble following Cash, having to trot from time to time to catch up. Noble had long legs and walked slowly, while Cash had a fast, choppy walk and gained ground every few minutes. Because he followed so comfortably, Mandy was able to look on both sides, remembering the little girl was wearing a bright blue tee shirt and pink shorts and shoes.

She felt very safe with Colonel Paul. She believed that he was highly trained for his work in the Army, and everyone could see that he was always aware of everything going on around him. He didn't talk much, and he moved quietly, confidently, yet humbly.

She heard something at the same split second that Cash and Noble both halted abruptly, ears perked, heads turned slightly to the right. Cash backed into Noble, who simply took a couple steps backward. She had never heard a rattlesnake before, but she was pretty sure that noise could be one. Timber rattlesnakes were abundant in Pennsylvania, though usually in the more mountainous regions. About 25 feet on the other side of the noise, Marina sat crying. One pink shoe was missing, and she was clutching a plastic bubbles bottle.

Colonel Paul swiftly dismounted and signaled Mandy to do likewise, not speaking out loud. He removed Cash's bridle, again hand signaling Mandy to do the same. He backed Cash toward Noble and Mandy moved the tall horse accordingly. Mandy copied Colonel Paul as he took the lead rope and tied it with a very loose slipknot to a tree. He motioned for Mandy to take the bridles and move over in front of the trees where the horses were tied.

The little girl saw Colonel Paul step back up on the path, and she started to stand up. "Marina, I am a friend of your grandfather," he said fluently in Spanish. "Stay very quiet right now. Do not move, little one. Do not move." He gestured a push with one hand, like asking her to sit back down. He put his finger to his lips for quiet, then smiled and nodded and pulled his finger across his mouth like a zipping motion. She had to stay still and quiet.

He knew that in the next minute the horses would spook, the girls would scream, and he better be dead on accurate.

Chapter

19

Colonel Paul moved slightly up the narrow forest road for a better visual on the snake, which began rattling again. Quicker than Mandy could have counted to three, Colonel Paul removed his sidearm from a shoulder holster under his shirt, took aim and fired. The horses spooked, the girls screamed, and the snake was dead.

"Mandy," he said quietly, "please carefully go down the hill over there, away from the dead snake, and get the little girl."

Mandy put the bridles on a tree branch and forced her shaking legs to move, while Colonel Paul calmed the horses. Noble had jumped but was not untied. Cash bolted, and the lead rope came undone. He stopped about 20 feet down the path from Noble. He looked back when Colonel Paul said his name, and he stood still until the man came for him.

Mandy came up carrying Marina. Her right foot was bleeding in a couple places, and she was clinging to Mandy and crying about her bubbles having spilled, though Mandy did not understand anything she said. They walked a short ways down the trail to a big rock, where

Colonel Paul suggested they rest for a few minutes.

Manuel and the women with Big Dan and Danny screamed when they heard the gun shot, then Big Dan's cell phone rang. He handed it to Manuel who started crying with the good news, and he spoke to Marina on the cell phone.

"We're going to rest a few minutes, then I'll walk the horses out on foot," Colonel Paul told him. "The girls will be on Noble, and I'll lead. We'll see you in about half an hour."

"We will walk your way," Manuel said. "See you soon. Gracias, Colonel Paul. Gracias, mi amigo. Gracias, mi Dios.

Colonel Paul untied the bag on the back of Cash's saddle and took out two bottles of water and a package of M&Ms and handed them to the girls. The crunch of the M&Ms package alerted Cash, but he didn't spook or move from where he was tied. He just looked concerned about the noise, which only lasted a moment.

From the first aid kit, Colonel Paul took some cleanser wipes, gauze and bandages. Gently, he cleaned the girl's foot examining it for splinters or any embedded material before wrapping it snugly. She was sitting on Mandy's lap, and she let Colonel Paul check her arms and legs for injuries. She had a small cut on her cheek that had dried. He asked Mandy to look carefully under her hair at her scalp for any blood or wound. He spoke to her sweetly in her language, and as long as she could cling to Mandy's arm, she was fine.

Mandy tightened her cinch and mounted, then Colonel Paul lifted Marina and set her in front of Mandy. There was room for both of them when Mandy scooted back in the saddle as far as she could, and she wrapped her arms around the little girl and held on the saddle horn as Colonel Paul would be leading them. He draped both bridles on either side of Cash's saddle horn, which at first startled the horse.

As Colonel Paul started leading both horses, Cash settled down, even walking more slowly than he did when he was being ridden. Mandy watched Cash and thought that he knew they were on a special mission, and he was supposed to walk very carefully. She thought about his sad eyes and wondered where he came from and what his life had been like that made him so scared. She was very happy that he moved to Amethyst Valley and shared a pasture with Noble, even though Noble was not near the upper fence and her hilltop hideout any more.

Mandy silently thanked God for His goodness, for finding Marina and for Cash and Noble and Colonel Paul. Her heart was especially warmed by the Colonel's confidence in her and Noble.

Twenty minutes later, the walking search party sighted them and started running up the dirt road, frightening Cash. He pulled at the lead rope and took a couple brisk steps sideways into some brush, which also startled him. Noble stopped and stood still. "Whoa, e-e-easy boy," said Colonel Paul in his smooth voice and even manner. He rubbed Cash's forehead and pulled his head slightly lower to relax him before proceeding.

The people slowed to a walk, and tears streamed down all the family members' faces at the sight of little Marina safely seated in Mandy's arms on the big, gentle giant horse. Back at the house, they offered thank yous and Manuel emptied his wallet of $82, but, of course, no one would take any money from him.

Colonel Paul took him aside and told him to come to see Natalie Adams next week. "She's a lawyer, Manuel. I had to tell her why I needed to borrow her trailer so quickly. She wants to see all your papers and make a list of who is here, and maybe she can help. You can trust her, mi amigo. She's one very sharp lady."

Manuel looked down at the ground. "I don't know how to thank you; what I can do for you?" he said. Colonel Paul touched his shoulder. "Would you have done the same for me if it had been my grandchild?" Manuel looked at him and nodded. Words were not necessary, and he returned to his family. The little search party loaded up and headed for home.

Kate was waiting at the farm when the trailer pulled in. She had called Martha for something and learned of the search. She looked concerned and walked straight to the driver's side door. Colonel Paul was surprised - and quite pleased - to see her. He assured her everyone was okay, and while he unloaded the horses, Kate helped Mandy with the tack. Mandy went home with her father and brother, while Kate stayed in the barn to brush down Noble and Cash and help Colonel Paul, whom she now called only "Paul."

He invited her into his cabin for the first time, and as she followed instructions to find something for them in the refrigerator, he unpacked the cantle bag. She said nothing when he took off his overshirt and carefully removed the shoulder holster and pistol. She found some soda, cheese, crackers, deli ham and pickles. She rolled the ham and arranged everything in a circle on a plate with one Milky Way Midnight Dark candy bar in the center, cut in two, and the pickles in a separate dish.

He had excused himself, and Kate took a look around the large, open room. The kitchen area was along the left wall, with the wood table sort of in the center of the back half. A brown tweed couch facing the wood stove separated the eating and living spaces. She smiled at the thought of him having hung the curtains, the package creases still in them.

The bookcase shelves were half full of books - classics by Charles Dickens and John Steinbeck, Western paperbacks and horse training and behavior titles. A small photo of an older couple standing in front of an adobe house was propped up against a small Indian vase. On the wall next to the bookcase was a framed cross stitch piece in navy blue thread:

Humility Comes Before Honor
Proverbs 15:33
LRS

Colonel Paul emerged from the bedroom in a clean shirt and walked over to her.

"LRS?" Kate queried.

"Lucille Ruth Silverton, my grandmother," he replied.

A light drizzle had moved in, and he closed the kitchen window. They sat at the table, and Colonel Paul told her of the day's events. They chatted about how hard it must be for families like Manuel's, so desperate for a decent life in a free country, possibly having risked their lives to get here and be together. Then they both fell silent, one of those frequent, quiet spaces in their friendship. He was thinking how fortunate he was to have been born on the U.S side of the border, and she pondered how small her issues seemed when compared to challenges that others, like Manuel and his family, faced.

Chapter

20

After an hour of snacks and cleaning up their few dishes, Kate said she needed to go home. She drew a deep breath, and asked if Colonel Paul would like to come over for dinner on Monday or Tuesday. She went on chattering that she knew he had to be at the farm most of the time and watch over everything, and it would be okay if he couldn't leave and ...

"Kate," said Colonel Paul quietly. "I'd like to come. What time?"

He had given Anne and Mandy a ride home once when a severe thunderstorm moved in unexpectedly. "If I recall correctly, it's that wickedly bright blue house."

"That's the one," she quipped. "I think it glows in the dark. Come at 6:00, we'll eat at 6:30."

"Okay," he said, "anything special I can bring? I make a great nachos dip, and I'll bring the chips, too."

Kate said that would be great.

He walked with her to the car, taking in everything to his right and left. He still had chores to do and a couple horses to get in, so they just exchanged a quick goodbye, and Kate drove away.

When she arrived home, Anne was sweeping the sidewalk and front steps, part of her weekly chores for a small allowance of $10. Neither heard the phone ringing until Kate opened the front door, trotting across the living room to answer it. It stopped ringing just before she reached it.

Over in Pittsburgh, Donna hung up, not sure if her sister had seen the caller ID and not answered, or if she wasn't home. She knew from their mom that Kate and Anne were settled in a cute, small house, painted an obnoxious shade of blue, and that Kate had new friends and was beginning to get out. She had circled an agoraphobic support group meeting in the newspaper for next Thursday evening at the county health clinic.

The next week at the Noble Spirit Horse Club meeting, they decided that Jennifer could sing the national anthem to open the show. Amanda would be the welcome announcer, though Mrs. Adams planned to do the events and announce winners for each class. Kerry said she had taken keyboard lessons, and she would practice every day and be able to play the national anthem perfectly for the show.

Others would be putting up flyers around town, taking the entry fees, stamping hands, helping groom and tack the horses they would use, handing out numbers to the competitors, and so on. The Wicked Three were true to their word and fit in nicely with everyone, not even sitting together at meetings.

A couple days later when Mandy was bringing fresh water buckets into the barn, she rounded the corner to find Natalie and an old woman in a wheelchair parked at the first stall door. Their backs were to Mandy.

"Well, I think this was Little Seed's stall," the seated woman was saying. "He was named for the little seed on his forehead. A handsome, reddish-brown, rust-colored Thoroughbred. He was a prize stallion, and he died of colic just before his third birthday. That was Captain Blue's stall," she continued, waving across the aisle. "He was a race horse, also a Thoroughbred, black with two stockings. Mommy always called him Midnight."

Mrs. Adams pushed the wheelchair forward, and the old woman consulted a drawing on a yellowed piece of paper. "What does this say?" she asked Natalie, who consulted the paper.

Chapter 20

"It says Suzy Q."

"Oh yes, this was Suzy Q's stall. She was Little Seed's mother, a quiet, gentle, brown mare." For the first time, Natalie noticed "Suzy Q" roughly carved into the wood above the door. "The middle stalls changed horses often, but this last one belonged to Garaitz, which means 'victory'. She was a Spanish mustang, the prettiest mare they ever owned and bred. A pewter gray horse with a thick forelock and long, silver mane that fell on the right side of her neck. She could take a blue ribbon just by prancing into a ring and looking at the judges."

The old woman hesitated and looked around. "Where's the pony?" she asked Natalie.

"I don't know," Natalie said. "Do you remember something? What color was he? What was his name?"

The old woman put her hand to her forehead and spoke in the present tense. "He is brown and white. He's mine. I call him Charlie. Is he here?"

Colonel Paul walked in the other end, and Mrs. Adams smiled at him. "Colonel Paul, I'd like you to meet my mother, Rosemary Bixler." It was too late to correct her slip-of-the-tongue. She meant to say just Rosemary.

The Colonel did a little double take at the name. "It's nice to meet you, ma'am," he said to the dull, blue eyes of the older woman.

"Have you seen Walter?" she asked.

Colonel Paul looked quizzically at Natalie, who told her that Walter died a long time ago.

"Well, when you see him," Rosemary continued, ignoring her explanation and speaking to Colonel Paul, "tell him the old wagon wheel is over there. It needs to be put back on the wagon."

Natalie and Colonel Paul followed her point to a dusty, large, wagon wheel leaning against the wall under the old grain dispenser.

"Sure, Mom," Natalie said gently. "We'll let him know the wagon wheel is here."

With that, she shrugged her shoulders and began pushing the wheelchair toward the house while the woman kept talking. "It seems like … something … Midnight won another race, and Charlie walked up on the front porch … Garaitz was left behind," she paused. "You're a nice lady to push my chair. Can we eat lunch now?"

Her mother had described it a million times, and Natalie

remembered all the horse stories her grandmother told her when she was a little girl. She handed the drawing to Natalie. "Do you want this old piece of paper?"

Mandy saw and heard it all. She and Colonel Paul exchanged glances, but neither said anything. She continued on her way to hang the water buckets inside the stalls, and he went to the tack room.

When Mandy got home, she told her mother about finding out that Natalie's mother's last name was Bixler and how she described the horses and stalls. "I know she has dementia," Mandy said. "But she seemed very certain about the horses. She knew their names and breeds and which stall belonged to which one. She had a drawing on an old piece of paper, and she talked about a paint pony named Charlie walking up on the front porch."

They sat together to do an Internet search. The second reference they clicked brought up a newspaper headline dated 70 years ago: "Bixler Family Hit with Tragedy." The subhead read: "town's founding family, children and all, vanish from farm." Big Dan and Danny came in, and they all turned attention to the newspaper article Martha and Mandy had just discovered when the phone rang.

"There's a fire at the Jackson house," someone said and hung up. They ran outside. Dan and Martha jumped into the front seat of the pick-up, while Mandy and Danny climbed in the back and held on to the sides.

Chapter
21

Winding through a few town streets, Big Dan rounded the corner onto Green Vine Lane. He couldn't get closer to the house than a block. They jumped out and ran over. Two fire trucks were spraying the back of the house, and the smoke stench in the air was wicked. There were two police cars, and paramedics were loading Mr. and Mrs. Jackson in the ambulance, despite their protests.

There was really nothing they could do. The fire was under control, and it appeared to have been contained to one back corner of the house. Not wanting to be a nuisance, they went home. Martha called Beverly Porter to get word out for food and whatever the Jacksons might need in the coming days. No one knew them very well. They were in their 60s and lived a very quiet life, going out every Sunday morning, probably to church. Someone had been picking them up in recent weeks, the neighbors said. And they were seen walking, hand in hand, to the grocery store on warm, sunny days.

Mr. and Mrs. Jackson asked that they be in the same curtained section in the emergency room, so the nurse on duty pushed two beds next to each other. Mrs. Jackson laid on one of the beds, and her husband sat next to her in a chair, holding her hand. They appeared to be praying when Dr. Gardner moved the curtain and walked in.

He paused until the man lifted his head and looked at him. "We're okay, Dr., really we are. Just a little coughing from the smoke."

"Well, well, let's just check your vitals and look you over anyway. We need to be thorough in cases of potential smoke inhalation. We are going to do some tests and check carbon monoxide levels," he said cordially, noting a nasty bruise on the man's forehead. He asked if that was from the fire, and Mr. Jackson said that he has dizzy spells. A couple days ago, he fell and hit his head on the side of a bookcase.

Indeed, his blood pressure and pulse were both lower than the doctor would want to see for a man in his mid-60s. He asked about their medical histories, medicines and so on. Neither said much, and neither one took medicine. They didn't have a family doctor. Mr. Jackson's shirt was worn through at the elbows.

Dr. Gardner ordered blood tests, as well as chest x-rays. He noted that the nurse had already recorded their heights and weights, and both were connected to blood pressure monitors. He thought they looked a little on the thin side. He'd send all the results to a local physician to follow up.

He didn't have time for more questions, as he heard the ambulance pull in and got word about three teens from a car accident, two with serious injuries. It would be five hours later when Dr. Gardner walked behind the admissions counter on his way out and noticed Mr. and Mrs. Jackson sitting in the waiting room.

"What are they still doing here?" he asked one of the clerks.

"I don't know," she responded. "They said they called someone to get them over an hour ago, but no one has come."

The doctor went to talk to them, then came back and called his wife, Carol. Thirty minutes later, she opened the door to let him in, trailed by the shy couple. Sam told her they were slender people, and she had laid out clean bathrobes, night clothes and slippers. The guest room looked like something out of a high class home magazine with its four poster queen bed, lavender and pale yellow matching drapes, upholstery and bed coverlet and luxury linens in its private bath on the left.

"This is lovely," stated Mrs. Jackson, setting her purse on the dresser. "Thank you so kindly. I'm sure we can go home tomorrow." Carol suggested they take a few moments, use the restroom and then come to the kitchen. "I bet you've missed supper. I have some beef stew ready for Sam, and there's plenty to go around. Come this way to the kitchen when you're ready," she gestured down the hall they had just walked through.

Mr. and Mrs. Jackson looked around the room, then she took from her purse a framed photo of a young girl, perhaps 12 or 13, and placed it next to the bed. They talked over supper about small stuff, assuring them that they were no trouble, and that the next day Carol would take them to their house and the police or fire department offices to find out when they could get back in.

"You can stay here as long as you need to, really. We don't have much company," she said, explaining that her family all lived in Spain, and the doctor's family was in Oregon. They did find out that church on Sunday was their only appointment, so to speak. "We'll all go," piped up Sam, telling them that driving two towns over in the next county was no big deal. The Jacksons exchanged glances and protested, but Carol agreed.

"I'm in, too," said Jennifer, who was happy that her mom and dad were getting along better. They talked a little more and were trying to do stuff as a family again, including going to church. All three of them silenced the Jacksons.

And that's how, on Sunday morning at 9:45, Sam, Carol and Jennifer Gardner found themselves in the fourth row from the front in the all-black Joyful Blessings Baptist Church in Garrison County. Sam estimated about 65 people there, and he figures he shook hands with every one of them. They were greeted and introduced to this person and that, all smiling, all joyful. The children stared and smiled at Jennifer. She was gorgeous and turned heads whenever she went somewhere new. Certainly, she was quite outstanding in this crowd with her creamy complexion and long, naturally blond, wavy hair.

If they felt at all out of place – and they did – at the beginning, the Gardner family felt overwhelmingly welcome by the end of the service. The minister asked all visitors to stand and introduce themselves. The family was among eight visitors that day, and during the prayer, each one was individually welcomed and prayed for.

Carol and Jennifer both marveled at the women's hats, and Sam noticed that the men – almost all in shirts and ties - sang with hands raised in the air along with the women. It was one of the most joyous church services they'd ever attended.

With all the pain and disaster that the physician saw in his line of work, he sometimes questioned a sovereign God of goodness and mercy. What he saw all around him on this morning was complete surrender, strong faith and unabated joyfulness. At the men's retreat he attended with Big Dan, he learned of the love of God, who sent his son, Jesus Christ, to die for our sins, so that everyone "who believes in Him shall not perish." He felt a special, spiritual presence and peace in that simple, but powerful, little church.

They spent the afternoon back at home, drawing out the Jacksons' life story over strawberry lemonade and a cold cut and cheese lunch outside on the main level deck. When Mrs. Jackson spoke, she inserted "the Lord God Almighty Himself" into almost every sentence. She was born and raised in Garrison County.

Mr. Jackson's grandfather had come up from the south to shoe horses at the farm that was now Amethyst Valley, and his grandmother worked in the big house as a cook and housekeeper. "There weren't a lot of opportunities for a black farrier in northern Mississippi before or during the Depression. The Bixlers were a wealthy family, made it in the coal business, I think. My father worked for them, too, until something dreadful happened. Almost overnight, the Bixlers were gone. The farm abandoned. I don't think anyone knows what really happened. There are lots of rumors, but I'm not repeating any of them. After that, my dad went into the floor business, and I worked with him after 12 years in the Navy. Anyway, I married Anna here, and we had a daughter, and I worked laying floors until just a few years ago. We've had a good life. My granddaddy built the house we now live in. We inherited it about 15 years ago and moved over from Garrison County."

Mrs. Jackson walked to the bedroom and returned with the framed photo from next to the bed. "This is our baby," she said.

"Naomi Hannah. We praise the Lord God Almighty Himself for her every day. We had 14 years of pure joy before He decided to take her home to heaven. We are so blessed for that. Her name means "beautiful grace," and she was remarkable, so energetic, so full of life. She was born with a heart defect, and we were told she might not live to age 3. Imagine our delight with 14 years!"

As she spoke, her eyes sparkled. There was no regret, no sadness about a life cut short, nothing but a face and voice filled with love. As if hearing Sam's inner astonishment at her radiance, she continued: "The Lord God Almighty Himself, He has His ways, and they are not always for us to understand, so we just hang tight to our faith and our memories. They're all glorious, aren't they?" She passed the photo to her husband, and he nodded, equally as happy, if just to gaze at the photo of their long-gone daughter. The doctor was thinking, at that moment, that the Lord God Almighty Himself had sent this couple to his home. Carol and Jennifer were thinking the same thing.

A Noble Spirit

Chapter
22

The Jacksons' small, 2-bedroom house reeked of smoke, and half the little town, it seems, had sprung into action. The Bible study ladies helped Mrs. Jackson take down all the curtains, pick up bedspreads, pillows and most of their clothes for cleaning. Martha took charge of all that because she knew a lot about fabric care. Some went to the laundromat, and some things she had dry cleaned; others she washed gently by hand at home.

Everyone in the Noble Spirit Horse Club showed up when she could and scrubbed walls and furniture. Carpet cleaners came to steam clean the rugs. Natalie Adams told Big Dan and Danny to take whatever they needed from the job site at her house, use it over there and replace it later. "A couple days' delay here won't make a big difference. Help the Jacksons get their home back in order," she'd said.

They just needed to replace one kitchen wall where the fire began. Old aluminum wiring, the fire chief had said. It started in an exterior wall, and thankfully, the smoke alarm in the kitchen alerted them before it could spread beyond one side of the room. A local electrician re-wired everything with copper and installed GFCI outlets throughout the kitchen.

Big Dan asked about the car in the back, noting that it had a current inspection sticker and license plates. Mr. Jackson said it quit running a few weeks back. "If I had some tools, I might could fix it," he said. Dan brought his tools the following day, and they worked together replacing the serpentine belt, along with the oil and oil filter for good measure. Soon the little blue Taurus was purring smoothly once again.

"You're quite handy with tools. You don't have any?" Dan asked. Mr. Jackson said he had to sell them to pay for his daughter's medical bills and never got around to replacing them. Martha and Beverly noticed the refrigerator and pantry were fairly sparse of food and staples. As the food rolled in from their church family at Joyful Blessings Baptist Church, as well as from neighbors, the grocery store, a local discount merchant, and the Bible study group, it overflowed everywhere. Mrs. Jackson's eyes filled with tears of gratitude, wondering where to put it all. Mrs. White said she had a big freezer, so she took some for storage.

One day, Big Dan brought Colonel Paul over to meet Mr. Jackson. They swapped some military service stories before the Colonel asked if he'd ever been to the VA hospital. No, he hadn't. "We don't take charity, you know," he said softly.

Colonel Paul understood that. He rolled up his left pant leg and showed him the plastic ankle piece and artificial foot. "I have an appointment in three weeks at the VA hospital. Why don't you come along? Dr. Gardner can forward your test results, and you can have an entire physical and evaluation at the same time I'm there. The hospital is there for us, Mr. Jackson. It's not charity. You have earned it by serving our country."

One week later, Mrs. Jackson folded the back stand on the framed photo of Naomi Hannah next to the bed in the Gardners' guest bedroom and returned home. The bungalow was clean and fully stocked. The car was full of gas, and there were no bills for anything. No one is sure who paid the carpet cleaners, painters, dry cleaners, electrician and others. "Well, I declare, the Lord God Almighty Himself knows," Mrs. Jackson said emphatically. "Sure enough, He knows."

A year later, Mrs. White was still delivering frozen food to the Jacksons. She was a widow who lived alone and enjoyed cooking again, neatly packaging servings for this couple with whom she had become close friends. She dined with them once or twice or three times a week and never tired of their always happy stories of Naomi Hannah.

Of course, Martha had invited Mrs. Jackson to the every-other-Wednesday ladies Bible study group and picked her up the following week. "We should all have a Bible like Mrs. Jackson's," she told Dan before crawling into bed that night.

"And what kind is that?" asked Dan, wondering what color the cover might be or what translation.

"Worn," Martha replied. "Frayed from use."

Dan smiled. His wife was right. He's not sure what he would have become if not for Martha and her infallible faith.

A new girl came to the next Noble Spirit Horse Club meeting. Sylvia Bannerwicz. Her mother came in with her and sat at the edge of the living room. She introduced herself as a homeschool kid, the oldest of three. "I'm 12, and I love horses, which was the only requirement on the flyer I saw at the library. We moved here two months ago to live on my grandparents' farm, and I have a horse. Well, there are three horses, and I call the paint mine but we all ride her. Her name is Painted Lady Two, and she goes by Lady. We have cows, chickens, 14 sheep and two dogs." Her face was bright and enthusiastic. Mandy glanced at Jennifer to be sure she wouldn't be rude. Jennifer caught the look and said, brightly and sincerely: "Nice to meet you, Sylvia, I'm Jennifer."

Kate explained to Sylvia how the meetings were run, and she called it to order. Mrs. White read the minutes, which were accepted. They began sharing what they learned or experienced since the last meeting before talking about helping the Jacksons and how that type of community spirit was part of their mission. Then they moved into more planning for the horse show.

Mandy had talked to her mom about making a special shirt for her to wear at the horse show. "Something aqua with sequins and fringe," she suggested. Being in the wedding and prom dress business meant Martha had lots of sequins, but certainly no western fringe, and nothing in cotton for a blouse. Mandy said her mother offered to make matching shirts for everyone if they could buy the fabric. She told them the color and showed them the design her mother had sketched. Because of the time constraint to make 12 blouses in a couple weeks, her mother suggested they skip the fringe.

"That's a great idea!" said Jennifer. "What about the same style and different colors. I look horrible in aqua." Leave it to Jennifer to be vain.

"I'd be happy to pay for the fabric, especially if I could have a red one and use it for other events. I think I'll enter a horse show at the agricultural complex in October," said Mrs. White. She was so cool, just as enthusiastic as the girls about horses and always sweet and encouraging. That's what made her a good teacher.

Martha would be going to the fabric store near the city in two weeks. She couldn't take everyone, so she suggested to Mandy that they all go to the hardware store, look at paint colors and mark two or three swatches they liked. Martha and Mandy would buy 3 yards of each fabric, as close to the colors as she could get.

Since the club was charging $3 per family and $1 per class entry, and Mrs. Adams said she didn't want the money, they decided to pay for thread, buttons and other supplies for their blouses from the club treasury after the horse show. Their meetings always adhered to Robert's Rules of Orders, and the group loved making motions and seconding them and voting. Mrs. White took notes and brought a typed copy of minutes to each meeting. Kate ordered an open-up folder with pockets for everyone as a small gift. Each one had horses on the outside, and the girls put in copies of the meeting minutes, flyers, notes on things they brought to share and other things they learned.

Also, at every meeting, besides sharing something they learned about horses since the last meeting, everyone was encouraged to share when she had embraced her "Noble Spirit." At this meeting, Mandy decided to tell everyone that it was her tallness and some of the kids' comments that made her invent the "Noble Spirit" in the first place.

She looked at Jennifer and smiled. When she was done, no one was angry. Kerry, Amanda and Jennifer just looked her way and mouthed "I'm sorry."

"It's okay," Mandy said cheerfully. "What if that didn't happen, and we wouldn't have the "Noble Spirit?" It's better this way, even though it hurt a little along the way. Mom says we're young, and we will get hurt lots of time in our lives. The really big times I needed it the most anyway was every time I thought Noble would be sold. That's the most scary thing I've ever experienced."

They talked about scary things for a while. Jennifer said her parents' fighting was the most scary for her, and how they were happier now. "I was afraid they'd get divorced and then Mom and I …" she stopped abruptly from saying "wouldn't have any money", realizing that Kate and Anne were in the room. She didn't want to hurt people's feelings any more.

Kate said it was time to move along the meeting. She was very sensitive to the girls and their various struggles. She seemed to know when to let the teenage talk roll along and when to step in to change the conversation or direction.

Mandy and Anne walked to the hilltop hideout after the meeting. They laid on the old beach towel and talked about the horse show. They agreed that Sylvia was neat, and Anne loved the idea for the shirt, saying hers would be pale yellow.

"Mandy, you have to keep this a secret, but I have to tell you. Colonel Paul came for dinner last week," Anne almost whispered, even though there was no one around for a mile, or at least half a mile.

"Wow," Mandy exclaimed. "They look so cute riding together. Well, Colonel Paul probably doesn't want to be cute, but, he is cute, don't you think?"

"Yes, he's handsome, I think, but I mostly like that he's smart and so good with the horses. I bet he had some bad stuff happen in the Army, too. I wonder if that's why he limps. But anyway, he brought nachos and a hot dip with cheese and chili. It was great. Mom cooked a beef stir fry. She let me bake biscuits for strawberry shortcake because we picked all those of strawberries early in the summer. Anyway, he's really nice, and we played a rummy card game he taught us. Progressive rummy. It was easy to learn and lots of fun. Mom won."

The next day was a Wednesday, and Mandy will never forget it. She did most of her work at the farm, then got Noble from the pasture. He was jumpy and kept looking behind him. His eye was way wide open, and he looked very frightened. He didn't pull away from her completely, but he spooked a few times on the lead and danced around her side and once in front of her. She got him to the barn and into the cross ties. He kept his head up high and moved from side to side whenever she tried to brush him or even touch him.

Mandy didn't know what to do, and she didn't see Colonel Paul anywhere. Mrs. White was riding in the arena, but it was too far away to shout at her. And what could she do anyway? So, Mandy clipped on his lead rope again, unhooked the cross ties and put Noble into Apache's stall. It was clean and had fresh water.

She ran to the cabin and knocked. Colonel Paul said "come in." He was working at a laptop computer on the rustic wood kitchen table. "Something is wrong with Noble," Mandy said, trying to steady her voice. "He's really scared, and he won't let me touch him or brush him. Please come look at him. Please come quickly, Colonel Paul. Something is wrong. I put him in Apache's stall."

Chapter
23

He got up, and they walked briskly, running part of the 30 yards between the cabin and barn. Colonel Paul went into the stall, and Mandy slid the latch tight. "E-e-e-easy boy, easy Noble, what's going on here big boy," he said in his usual calm, soft voice. It was obvious Noble was out of sorts, acting frightened. He also moved away at any touch and would not be calmed, though he didn't kick or bite or anything. He was restless and hypersensitive. Colonel Paul lifted each foot to check the hoof.

Colonel Paul came out. "You did the right thing, Mandy. Something is definitely not right. I'll call the vet."

During the next hour, Mandy worked as fast as she could filling the water tanks in the pastures, then sweeping the barn. She didn't want to clean the front porch or deck at the house because she wanted to be near the barn when the vet arrived. His dark green truck finally pulled into the driveway, and Mandy ran to the driver's side door.

Dr. Turney got out, and seeing the distress on the girl's face, he smiled, took a bag from a side compartment and said "Show me to your horse."

"He's not my horse, Doctor," Mandy said, "but he's my best friend and the love of my life, and I know he's not feeling good. He's really calm and gentle, but now he's scared of something, and I can't pet him or brush him."

Colonel Paul came in the other end of the barn at the same time. He'd met Dr. Turney once before, and he shook his hand and pointed to Noble. "He's hypersensitive and acting spooky," he explained. "He the most calm Thoroughbred I've ever seen, and I've seen lots of them. He doesn't really know the meaning of spooky, though I've only been here a few months now."

"I've seen Noble before. He's blind on the right, correct? Yes, here he is. Let's see what's going on here, big guy, let's see," he said, letting himself into the stall and trying to run his hand along his neck and shoulder. Noble moved away instantly. The vet was very thorough, taking all his vital signs, checking in his mouth, looking at his feet.

He asked Colonel Paul to come in with the lead rope and hold him so he could draw some blood for tests. He asked if anything had changed in his diet, pasture mates, changes in grazing, anything they had noticed, but neither Colonel Paul nor Mandy knew of anything, except Cash's arrival five weeks earlier.

"I rode him two days ago, just walking in the arena, and he seemed fine. Maybe, now that I think of it, a little more jumpy when I was leading him, but I didn't think anything of it, just that he noticed something I didn't see. Sometimes he jumps a tiny bit when something comes into his sight on the left side. I brushed him, and he was okay," Mandy related.

The vet did a little more checking and suggested that the blood tests would tell if he had Lyme disease. He explained that nearly a quarter of deer ticks now carried it, and hypersensitive skin was a symptom. They are as small as a pin head, so it's not something one would see even when he was brushed. He assured them that the horse could be out in the pasture. He knew an associate was going to the lab first thing in the morning, and he'd send along the vial with him instead of mailing it, so they wouldn't have to wait long for results. Maybe tomorrow afternoon. They'd test for Lyme, and if it turned out negative, they'd run tests to assess liver, kidney and muscle enzymes, as well as other tick borne diseases like erlichia or anaplasma.

Colonel Paul was holding Noble, and after the vet left, he led him back to the pasture he shared with Cash. Mandy wanted to put her arms around his neck and lean against him and stroke him like she did so often, but she knew he wasn't comfortable being touched right now. She went to the house to do the patio and porch cleaning with tears just rolling down her cheeks.

When she was done, she took apple pieces to Noble. He didn't run from her, but he didn't put his head down for his forehead to be rubbed either. She didn't try to pet him, and she told him she would pray for him and think about him all night long, and that she'd stay with him day and night if it would help.

Her father and brother were there weekdays, along with his friend, Assan, and Rachel's boyfriend, Andy. They were the construction crew for the little apartment. The half basement had been dug out and foundation poured. They planned to build most of the apartment and get the roof on before opening up the house wall to connect the two. Today they were starting on the sub floor. The plan was for completion a week before the horse show, so Natalie could furnish it, and people could see it.

Mandy walked over and told them all about Noble. "I'm sorry, sweet pea," said her dad, placing an arm around her shoulders. "The vet will know what to do when he knows what the problem is. Do you want to help us here?" She nodded and walked around picking up any papers or debris on the ground, as well as swinging a large magnet on the bottom of a pole for nails and any metal. Big Dan insisted that the job site be as clean as possible at all times.

Mandy got on her knees next to the bed that night. "Dear God. It's Mandy. Noble is sick, and we don't know what's wrong yet. Please please let the vet know what it is and how to treat him, and please heal him. I know you know what will happen, and I know you hear my prayers, even though I'm just a teenager. I love you, and I believe in you, and I hope you will please heal Noble quickly. I want to ride him in the horse show, God. Thank you. Love, Mandy. Amen."

Mandy woke up at 5 a.m. There was no point in going to the farm yet. She didn't work today anyway, but she'd go at lunch time, even though she knew Colonel Paul would call her as soon as he heard anything. She fell back asleep for an hour, then went downstairs for some juice and cereal before going back to her room and pulling out her "Noble Spirit" folder. She kept the meeting minutes and other notes in here. She had started a poem about the "Noble Spirit," and she read what she had so far:

It's the inner courage you draw on
When you're running life's race,
And someone's making you unhappy.
Someone is in your face.
You think of this horse alone
Standing in a pasture half blind;
Standing tall, standing strong
Being brave, and staying kind.

When the others run him away,
He turns and walks alone.
When they bite and nip at his side,
He moves away from harm.
He holds his head up high
And looks with his one good eye.
He carries himself with pride
And relies on what's inside.

Colonel Paul called at 11:20 a.m. The vet confirmed that Noble had Lyme disease, and he would come at 2 p.m. Mandy called Anne, then she ate an early lunch, met Anne at the hilltop hideout and walked to the farm to tell Noble. She went through the fence with a few carrot pieces, which didn't interest him this time. He stood still for her, and she didn't try to touch him. She talked to him, and she and Anne sang to him as he grazed. Colonel Paul once said it's always a good sign if a horse is grazing, so that was an encouragement.

Mandy went to the barn for his lead rope and told Colonel Paul she would have it at the pasture gate, knowing he preferred to lead Noble when he might be jumpy. He was the same as yesterday, frightened and looking around and behind him. They put him again in Apache's stall until the vet arrived.

"We've caught it early," Dr. Turney said, "so I expect he will respond well to treatment. I will shave here on his neck and give him an intravenous injection once a day for 28 days. He should have a full recovery."

Mandy was so relieved, and the girls watched as the vet shaved a section about the size of a deck of cards on the left side of Noble's neck. Colonel Paul held him as the needle went in, and the doctor held it for nearly five minutes.

"It's a slow release injection," he explained. "This drug can cause complications when given too fast, so we put the medicine in slowly."

"When can I brush him or ride him again?" Mandy asked. The vet suggested she wait a couple days before trying to brush him and perhaps she could ride him lightly in a week, just walking for half an hour to start. "Do you think I can ride him in the horse show in five weeks?" she inquired.

"I do," said the vet, "but it's a day by day evaluation in these early days." They agreed to have Noble in Apache's stall every day at 10 a.m. The vet would come between then and 1 p.m. to give the shot, then he could be turned out again. "We need to watch the injection site for heat or swelling. Mandy, can you wipe it every day with gauze and a little antiseptic before and after the shot? I can leave you the supplies, and I'll show you what to do right now."

And so, every day, Mandy was there at 9:30. Colonel Paul led Noble the first three days, but he responded so well to the medicine that the fearfulness was gone in three days, and Mandy could lead him and brush him softly again. She checked his feet every day, picking his hooves and brushing them with hoof conditioner every other day because it was dry weather.

The horse club members planned to come almost every day the first week in August to begin practicing for the horse show. Kate and Mrs. White volunteered to supervise, as Colonel Paul had his regular work and training sessions. Natalie Adams was there part of the time and at the house part of the time. She was in the process of moving her office to her home, so there were lots of boxes and office furniture being unloaded from a big truck and taken into the house on Wednesday. She had two employees who could do most of the office organizing.

As promised, Natalie brought Kazi to the barn and introduced her to Jennifer, who had her heart set on entering with her in the horse show. "She can be a little spirited," Natalie warned her. "You can lead her and see how it goes." Jennifer did fine, and Kazi was on her best behavior. Because she had entered so many trail competitions, the Arabian was not frightened of much. She'd had those Styrofoam swimming pool noodles in her face and a tarp over her head. She would walk through mud, over poles or across a narrow wood bridge. Arabians are famous for endurance in all kinds of weather and geographical conditions.

Mandy asked Colonel Paul if she could begin riding Noble at the beginning of the second week of his treatment. "Maybe I can get on bareback, so he's not bothered right away with the saddle and cinch tight on his skin?" she suggested. He agreed. She brought Noble to the round pen, and he brought the bridle. Of course, he knew she could get on from the fence, so he just watched.

The gentle giant was as calm as ever once again, and she began to walk him in circles and figure eights using just her legs and seat for signals. She had the bridle on, but refrained from steering with the reins, to see how we responded to just leg cues. She would lean slightly forward to walk, then sit straight up, and sit a tiny bit back, take in a big breath and let it out, saying "whoa" when she wanted Noble to stop. He behaved perfectly.

Mandy was especially happy to once again feel the soft warmth of his back, his muscles gently moving as he walked around. After a few days, she moved to riding him in the arena.

Natalie was an expert rider and jumper, and she decided to try Noble over a couple small jumps. She wasn't, however, a bareback rider, and tacked him with one of her English saddles. The girls watched excitedly as she warmed up Noble before heading him into two short jumps. Noble did everything flawlessly, and she jumped him again. Two days later, Natalie supervised Mandy's first bareback jump.

Everyone clapped, and Colonel Paul saw it all from where he was working in the round pen with Cash. He just smiled. "There's no holding her back, Cash," he said to his horse. "She's a natural horse girl through and through."

The horse club kept meeting every Tuesday. The girls had different schedules of practicing with the horses, and by the middle of August, Kate developed the final horse show program. Amanda brought her keyboard to one meeting, and she and Jennifer performed the national anthem and a huge surprise.

Mandy had added more to her Noble Spirit poem the morning she was waiting to hear about Noble's illness from the vet. She shared it with the group the week before, and Jennifer and Amanda took it to Mrs. Engels for help with music. Everyone was awestruck at the result – a song of strength set to a snappy tune that made their hearts soar at the sound. Mrs. Engels used part of her addition as the chorus.

Later that afternoon, Mandy and Anne invited Jennifer to the hilltop hideout after the meeting. Mandy pulled out the old beach towel, and they lined up on their bellies and elbows overlooking the horse farm.

"So, how do you always stay so nice to everyone, Mandy?" Jennifer asked.

"Oh, I don't. Trust me. Last year I told off a girl in my gym class who bugged me so much. When I told my mom about it, and I said 'she deserved it,' my mother said no one deserves ill words. She was going to drive me to her house and make me apologize, but I wouldn't get in the car. When my dad came home, he was really mad. He said if I didn't get into the car in five minutes, he'd put me in it. Well, you've seen my father. He could do it. I got in, and my mother drove, and my father sat like a guard in the back seat."

Mandy took a breath. "When we got there, I walked into the most awful smelling, dirty house I've ever seen. I told the girl I was sorry in front of her mother, who was wearing pajamas and smoking. At home, Dad said to eat my supper and go to my room, but I just went to my room. I read once that you can live longer without food than water, so when I got hungry, I drank water in the bathroom upstairs."

"Wow," Jennifer said. "You do get into trouble sometimes?"

Mandy nodded. "Oh, yeah. I learn a lot from my mother, but you can only imagine sometimes how annoying she is - always quoting from the Bible. My grandfather is a Baptist minister, and my mother lives by God's Word. But, ya know, she's usually right. Well, she always right. Even that night, I felt better for apologizing to the girl, but, I didn't tell my parents that."

"I was 7 ½ when my father left us, and I don't know why my mother wasn't mad. He just moved out one day while we were at my Grandma's house," Anne said.

"And your mother didn't get angry?" Jennifer asked.

"No, she just cried a lot. I got kicked out of school last year because some kids said my mom was a crazy nut, and probably I was crazy, too. We were in the library, and I picked up some books from the table and threw them at the kids."

"I bet your mom was mad at that?" Mandy suggested.

"Well, she couldn't drive to the school by herself, so one of my uncles came for me. He's really cool, and he loves us a lot. He laughed about it all the way home, saying we're all a little crazy in different ways. But, you're right, Mom didn't think it was at all funny. I had to stay home for three days, and Grandma took her to meet with the principal. I think that's when she decided we'd move near my Aunt Donna. When that didn't work out, she told me: 'We are going to make it on our own, Anne. You and me, against the world, if that's what it takes.'"

"It's sort of cool to know you guys aren't perfect," Jennifer sighed.

"Oh, definitely not," said Mandy.

"Mom says if you keep a bitterness toward someone, it grows inside you, and the person most hurt is yourself," Anne stated, "and that's why she wouldn't be mad at my father. He doesn't even send us money. She says if she took him to court, the lawyers would end up with more money than we would. Grandma sends money sometimes. I was angry with her for not coming to my school play two years ago. She's really trying hard now, and I'm so happy we moved here. It's the first time that I've lived in a house, not an apartment."

"I hang out with Amanda and Kerry becuz it's so lonely and quiet and boring at my house," Jennifer chimed in. "We don't have any neighbors. Kerry's mother is really cool. Very laid back. She's got three younger brothers and three big dogs, and the house is always a busy, cheerful place to be. Our house used to be fun, a long time ago."

Her voice quivered on the last sentence, and Mandy put her hand over Jennifer's, a comforting gesture she'd so often received from her mom. "I think God made the Jacksons stay with us and talk about their daughter," Jennifer began. "My little brother died a week before his 5th birthday from eating a poisonous mushroom on a hike. I was 6. Dad was mad because Mom wasn't watching him closely, and Mom was angry because Dad couldn't save him. After that, Dad started working all the time, and Mom just hung around depressed, no longer doing her art or volunteering or talking about having more children. Sometimes it felt like I didn't matter any more to them. And up until Mr. and Mrs. Jackson's visit, no one talked about him."

Jennifer stopped, and Mandy and Anne waited. "After they went home, my parents got out some family photos with Little Ben, and we shared memories, and we all cried and laughed, and Mom suggested we celebrate his birthday every year. Dad asked us to hold hands, and he prayed that we always be thankful that we had Little Ben, even for a short time. They cried and held me so tightly that I thought they'd crush me, but it felt really good. It's like a big, heavy cloud was lifted off our house."

"My mother says Jesus can get us through anything," said Mandy. "And now we have the 'Noble Spirit'! She found a place in the Bible where the word 'noble' appears three times in one sentence."

"Where?" Anne asked.

"How should I know?" Mandy responded. "Go ask my mother if you want to know where something is in the Bible."

They all giggled. And a special bond of friendship took root.

Words
By Sue Cameron
[www.grammysue.com]

Is there anything more powerful?
To heal, to hurt,
To destroy?
Words in my mind – accusing me,
Dragging me down
Into guilt and helplessness.
Words from outside – attacking me,
Tearing at the fragile image of who I am and hope to be.
I struggle under their heavy weight
And fear I'll suffocate.
Not all words are true, but they feel true.
Some are lies wrought in the basement of hell,
Sent to defeat those who march in the army of God.
My Leader warned me of such warfare,
So subtle and hard to detect.
A sudden attack strips my defenses.
Wounded, bleeding,
I am left to die.
Now my fate depends on
To whom I choose to listen.
To the liar,
Or to my Leader.
His Word consoles and strengthens me,
Binding my pain and wrapping me in acceptance.
He does not condemn me in my weakness,
Or require me to run on broken legs.
He asks only that I listen to him
And believe what he says.
His truth banishes falsehoods
And sets me free.
Living on the battlefield isn't kind and gentle;
It is demanding and stretching.
I must often pause and ask myself,
To whose voice do I listen?
And in whose voice do I speak?

~ ~ ~

~ reprinted by permission ~

154

Chapter
24

Kate had to stop taking entries into all the classes. They had a limit of 12 horses per class, and the news of the show had spread by flyers and word of mouth over several counties. They supposed there weren't many casual horse shows for kids and regular riders, and everyone was surprised and pleased with the interest. They projected maybe 50 people and hoped for as many as 15 riders, including club members.

Martha worked day and night on the Noble Spirit blouses, and she had them done one week ahead of the show. Kate, with help from Danny's friend Assan, had designed a Noble Spirit patch. In addition to being skilled in drawing software, he was a talented artist.

Martha sewed one on each upper, right sleeve. "It goes on the right arm to remind you to do the right thing in situations where you have a choice," she had explained. Mandy added that Noble was blind on the right.

Everyone was ecstatic. Jennifer was the only one who chose white. "To match Kazi," she said. She had mounted and walked Kazi around the arena 100 times, and she couldn't wait to join the competition. Mandy offered Noble to Anne and a couple other girls. He would be entered in almost every class. Anne was riding Checkers twice. Sylvia, Mrs. White, Rachel and Razia were riding their own horses, and Mrs. Adams' Appaloosa, Paloosa, was on loan for Kerry and Amanda. Mandy planned to ride her once or twice, too. They had practiced a lot at the walk and trot, and all the horses were well-trained, reliable steeds and would be tacked in Western saddles. But, of course, they were still horses. "There's no such thing as a bombproof horse," Mrs. Adams told them more than once.

The Friday before the horse show was Mandy's 15th birthday. The previous Tuesday, Kate made and decorated a yummy carrot cake for her, which was served at the Noble Spirit Horse Club meeting. On Friday her mom planned a small dinner party at home with Kate and Anne, Colonel Paul and the Gardners. Her parents gave her a black, leather bridle with matching reins and a snaffle bit, and Danny's present was a new, aqua and black halter and matching lead rope.

Mandy thanked them, figuring she could use them on Noble sometimes. Jennifer had purchased a padded saddle pad with a black, white and aqua pattern. Mandy was ecstatic and already hoped that Colonel Paul wouldn't mind if she brought these things to the barn. She thought of an empty hook in a corner of the tack room. Kate and Anne's gift was a beautiful, framed photo of Noble and a pretty, sequined belt. She knew right away she would wear it for the show.

Colonel Paul handed her an envelope. "A nice birthday card," she supposed. And it was a pretty card with a horse on the front and Happy Birthday in blue script. Inside was a folded piece of paper. Mandy thought right away it was a little check. She opened it and read:

Will you be a one-half, co-owner of Noble with me?
Your friend, Colonel Paul
(P.S. This present will actually cost you: $25/month)

The room was silent. She read it again. She looked at her parents.

"You know about this?" she asked.

"Yes, and you can call Noble your horse," her father replied.

She smiled at Colonel Paul. "Your first horse," he said lightly with a smile.

"Thank you is not even enough," Mandy stated.

"You've worked all summer, even on days you weren't paid," the Colonel explained. "You've proven yourself to be a natural horse person, a hard worker, sensible, willing to learn. As long as Noble is part mine, he can live at Amethyst Valley free. Your monthly contribution will go toward semi-annual check-ups and shots, hoof supplements and winter grain. There might be a time or two that Mrs. Adams or I use him for a lesson. And, we hope Kate can ride him so, you know, so we can, um, check the fences and the new trails your father is cutting on the other side." Everyone at the barn loved watching Colonel Paul and Kate ride together.

"Absolutely, absolutely," Mandy said. Her heart was so full, she couldn't think of anything else to say. She picked up the framed photo and hugged it tightly to her chest.

"Noble," she whispered. "You're partly mine, my gentle giant. Thank you, thank you all so much. What an amazing birthday; what an awesome summer!"

Big Dan, Danny, Assan and Andy worked tirelessly to have the little apartment addition completed a week before the horse show. All the subcontractors showed up on time, and the entire little project was fast becoming a huge success. Every night, Big Dan and Danny, sometimes with the others, had gone over every detail of the day, reviewed the next steps and talked about materials and supplies and anything they needed.

As Big Dan bought new tools, he saved his old ones. One day, he stopped at the shop and asked Mr. Morton if he had any tools he wasn't using. His old boss pointed to a bin in the far corner. "Take anything from there that you can use," he said. Big Dan lifted and looked at every one, taking 14 items. He gave them, along with things he didn't need any more, to Mr. Jackson who assisted with flooring decisions and supervised the installation.

Natalie Adams ordered all the furniture in advance, and it was sitting in plastic in the big house living room and hallway. On Wednesday before the show, the men laid a large Persian rug in the great room, then brought in the furnishings.

The every-other-Wednesday ladies Bible study group came to iron and hang curtains, put dishes and utensils in the cupboards and help Natalie ready the space for her mother's move on Friday. Her husband, Matthew, would be back on Saturday from an intensive summer of flying overseas and spending time with their daughter in Switzerland. She wanted everything in good shape for both of them. There were still some interior renovations to be done, but the house was warm and inviting, and she was beside herself with joy at how the farm was taking shape.

Knowing that this was Big Dan's first construction project, Natalie also wanted the apartment finished so people could tour it and see his workmanship. They used all local contractors and a local cabinet maker. She purchased everything she could at stores in Bixlerville. She only had to order the kitchen tile and the stackable washer and dryer from outside the county. She was delighted with the finished living space.

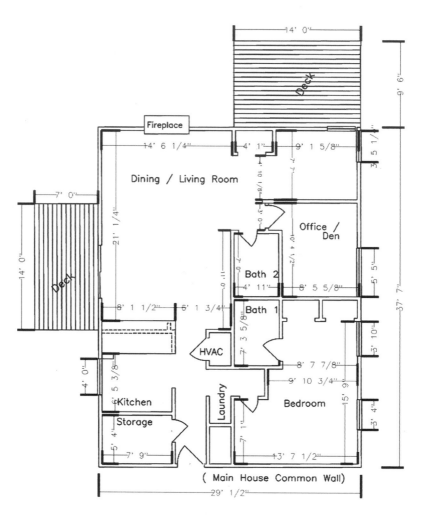

Rosemary's Apartment

Chapter
25

The day of the Noble Spirit Horse Club Show dawned with a clear, blue sky and sunshine, an autumn crisp in the air and the characteristic greens of summer yielding to the traditional colors of fall. Club members arrived around 8 a.m., and the show was set to begin at 11:00.

The Adamses had a section of fencing in the front pasture next to the road taken out. Manuel Perez had come over a couple times to show Danny and his buddies the best way to remove and re-install the fence sections. The horse trailers and trucks could easily park there and not crowd the grounds around the house and arena.

Danny and his friends gathered at 7:00 a.m. to go over their responsibilities and put on lime green vests on loan from Big Dan's buddy at the state highway department. The first truck and horse trailer arrived just before 9 a.m. They expected maybe a dozen horse trailers and directed at least two dozen by 10:15, with a few more to come.

Aluminum, rented bleachers had been moved in and assembled

the day before, providing seating for around 100. The little horse farm was abuzz with activity as horses and ponies of all shapes and sizes were unloaded and walked around the grounds in the roped off section "for horses only, no one mounted." People started filling the bleachers.

The Porter family arrived with the baby twins in their double stroller. Mrs. Engels and lots of the teachers and school people showed up. Mr. Morton brought his grandchildren, and families and children and older folks crowded on to the horse farm.

Mr. and Mrs. Jackson arrived with five children, all in cowboy hats, neck kerchiefs and sunglasses. Jennifer noticed them right away and figured they were kids from their church, not actually looking at them very closely. She'd go say hi later. The little girls had been so sweet that day her family attended the morning service. One of them had asked if she could touch her hair. Jennifer waved, but they didn't see her.

Manuel Perez showed up with his family in his pick-up truck and a car, and Marina bounced over to the judging booth to find Mandy. Manuel looked for Colonel Paul. "We'll see them later," the grandpa said. "I'm sure they're here somewhere. Let's go get seats. Mama and Grandmama are delivering food to the big house, and the rest are over there."

Officer Reggie Cole watched Manuel from his patrol car parked next to the ambulance. He got out and stepped into his path.

"Señor Perez?" he asked.

Manuel's heart leapt into his throat. He instinctively picked up Marina. "Sí, señor. I am Manuel Perez." Instantly, he wished he had spoken totally in English.

"We were talking about you at the station yesterday." He paused. "Did you do all these fences?" Manuel nodded. "Nice work. Well, the chief's wife wants some decorative fence in her front yard. I need an underground invisible fence for my dogs around an acre and half. Do you do those?"

The lump in his throat retreated. "Yes, sir, I can sink an invisible fence for dogs and show you how to train them," he stated slowly.

"Well, if I can get your phone number or you have a business card …" the officer responded, taking his patrol pad from his chest pocket.

Manuel set down Marina and reached for his wallet. He was acutely aware that when he opened it, his legal Pennsylvania driver's license was in the clear pocket. He pulled out two business cards, pleased that he had ordered them only a month ago.

"Well, they're a bit crumpled, but my phone number and my e-mail address are on them. I can give you a quote when you're ready," he said.

"Thanks. Enjoy the show," responded the policeman, just as his shoulder radio speaker squawked at him about some loose dogs on the other side of town. He walked away, and Manuel caught Colonel Paul's concerned look from the arena. He gave a thumbs up, and the Colonel nodded. By this time, the women had returned, and seats were filling fast. "Aquí, aquí, muchacha," his wife said to Marina, who took her hand and walked to a bench where other family members had saved some space.

One man arrived alone in a white Chevrolet Tahoe with Colorado license plates. He wore a Philadelphia Eagles ball cap, lightweight navy blue sweater, dress slacks and wingtip shoes - the $600 Italian variety - and top of the line, designer sunglasses. He strolled over to the bleachers and inconspicuously took a seat next to Mr. and Mrs. Jackson and their little entourage.

Kate watched the stands fill to overflowing. She noticed one lady with a large, floppy hat and smiled to herself, thinking about the times she and her sister would outlandishly decorate hats every spring for their Kentucky Derby Day Party. A hat would come in handy on this sunny day, too.

Ten minutes before the show was to begin, neither Colonel Paul nor Mandy could be found anywhere. "Have you seen Paul?" Kate asked Big Dan. "Oh, he'll be around soon," he responded casually. Kate suspected something was up, but couldn't figure out what and didn't have time to think much about it.

Jennifer, Kerry and Amanda had been at the horse farm three days in a row, practicing their announcing and music, getting comfortable with the microphones and their participation in two surprises - one at the beginning and one at the end. Mrs. White and Razia collected the entry fees and stamped a horseshoe on the back of everyone's hand. Natalie was in charge of getting all the riders and parents, if the rider was under 18, to sign the waivers she prepared and answer questions.

Martha, Beverly and the Bible study group ladies coordinated all the food, which seemed to flow unabated on to tables under a large, rented tent. Just outside one end of the tent stood a covered wagon about the size of an SUV, and next to it, huge black kettles would warm the pork barbecue and baked beans over real fires. The canvas sides of the covered wagon were rolled up and five gallon containers for lemonade and iced tea were set up along one side. Paper plates, cups, plastic utensils and napkins sat nearby, ready to be opened after the show.

Volunteer judges had been lined up. An ambulance with paramedics was parked near the arena, and Big Dan would man the gate, letting horses and riders in and out before and after each class. It was like the whole town and most of the county came out to support the little horse club, see the farm renovation and enjoy the spectacular autumn day. Amethyst Valley Bible Church had a booth giving out free water with a sign and Bible verse about the water of life.

When the bleachers were filled and overflowing, people with lawn chairs set them up, and others stood near the fence. There had to be more than 200 people and at least 25 trailers, and some trailers had two horses. Razia and Sylvia brought their horses. Of course, Mrs. White and Rachel would compete on Harmony and Apache. Noble, Kazi, Paloosa and Checkers were saddled and waiting in the round pen.

The Noble Spirit Horse Club blouses – each one in a different color – were hanging neatly in the tack room. Some members put them on as soon as they arrived. Mandy, Anne and a couple girls who groomed and tacked the horses put theirs on just before the show.

Amanda played a medley of contemporary rock while people settled into a viewing spot or groomed, saddled and walked horses. Dr. Gardner checked in with the local paramedics, and he and Carol sat with them, since there wasn't any space left in the bleachers.

Things didn't get started at 11:00 as anticipated, but at 11:20, Amanda played very loudly on the keyboard to get everyone's attention. Jennifer stood at the microphone in her white, Noble Spirit Horse Club blouse with a purple print kerchief at her neck, her wavy blond hair falling around her shoulders in the breeze. Amanda tested the microphone and began speaking:

Welcome. Hello. Welcome. Welcome everyone to the first Noble Spirit Horse Club Show at Amethyst Valley. She paused as people stopped talking and turned their attention. *My name is Amanda, one of the club members. Will you please stand for our national anthem which will be sung by Jennifer Nichols, accompanied on the electronic keyboard by Kerry Wilson, both also members of the Noble Spirit Horse Club. Please everyone, sing along. Then remain standing for the opening prayer, which will be delivered by Pastor David Porter.*

People stood up and looked around for an American flag. Amanda waited until voices quieted. Spectators and participants sort of gazed at the vacant arena. Kerry played a couple chords and halted. Amanda spoke when Big Dan opened the gate. Mandy led Cash and Colonel Paul into the arena and stepped aside.

A Noble Spirit

Chapter
26

Our flag bearer today is Lieutenant Colonel Paul Robert Silverton, retired, of the U.S. Army Special Forces. He moved to Bixlerville five months ago after 20 years of active duty, to be the general manager at this horse farm. He proudly wears the blue dress uniform of the Army and a plethora of commendations including the Silver Star, an award for heroism, and a Purple Heart for wounds in combat while serving our country in Afghanistan. His mount is named Cash, and he is a Belgian pony cross also retired from the Army.

His profile was most similar to a Belgian, and who needed to know that Cash sort of flunked out of the Army in three days? The crowd applauded and waved their hats, which, of course, spooked Cash. Colonel Paul kept him busy trotting figure 8s and doing circles instead of going around the edge of the arena as he'd planned and practiced. Getting too close to the crowd would be challenging for this horse he'd grown to love so much.

A 3 x 5-foot American flag anchored into a flag stand on the right side of the saddle furled as they moved. Colonel Paul abandoned the 4 x 6-foot flag he first tried in their practice sessions. At one point, he thought he'd have to carry a tiny, two-inch flag in his hand!

Cash was obviously nervous with Old Glory so close to him and all the hooplah from the stands, jigging sideways while trotting faster and faster. Colonel Paul did his best to calm him with his steady voice, though he wasn't sure Cash could hear him. Stabilizing the wood flag pole with his right hand and holding the reins in his left hand meant he had no way to stroke his withers, another calming method for the horse. He just kept turning him this way and that; no doubt, the spectators thought it was all part of their act.

Finally, the noise subsided, the horse quieted down a little, keeping his right eye on that flag, still waving slightly in the warm, fall breeze. Colonel Paul took a deep breath and released it and waited. Cash did the same, his sides expanding, then releasing. The Colonel nodded to Kerry.

She played a few introductory chords before Jennifer's clear voice began "Oh-h, say can you see, by the dawn's early light, what so proudly … "

People started singing along and by the end of the anthem, Mandy was sure it could be heard to the end of State Highway 24, some 50 miles away. She had convinced Colonel Paul to do this, hesitant though he was to flaunt his bravery ("just following orders," he'd said) or service record. Cash stood perfectly still, even lowering his head when Colonel Paul ever so lightly lifted the right rein with one finger while still holding the flag pole. Everyone bowed for the opening prayer for fun and safety and God's blessing on the day and the community.

As the crowd sat down, and the noise died down, Colonel Paul did trot Cash, flag and all, once around the inside perimeter of the arena. Big Dan opened the gate, and Mandy led them away. The Colonel had not wanted to mount or dismount in front of the spectators. He did not want to illicit any curiosity about why he did so on the right hand side of his horse, sometimes taking a few seconds to hear the click of the magnet on the bottom of his left boot.

Horses and riders lined up neatly for the first event, while Natalie took to the microphone, explaining how the show would be structured. All participants had received detailed rules of the show, and she reminded them again that if horses spooked or any incident occurred, and they fell off, they were not to worry about their horse. She had Mandy, Colonel Paul, the judges and Kate prepared to enter the ring and catch a loose horse or assist riders. Riders who stayed on their horses during any incident were to steer them directly to the closest fence section and stand still.

She introduced the three judges – an uneven number, so there would be no tie for places. Two were veterinarians from UPENN, the veterinary school at the University of Pennsylvania, and the other was a horsewoman friend of Natalie's who competed all over the country in a wide variety of equine events. The veterinarians were also on standby in case a horse was injured.

The first class was an open halter class (no age specification) where each entrant would simply lead a horse, stopping, walking and turning as Natalie, who served as show event announcer, called out. Anne led Noble. Jennifer led Kazi. A little girl about 5 led a Shetland pony. She wore a white blouse, tan rider pants, tall, black boots and had braids with pink ribbons. The butterscotch colored pony had pink ribbons in its mane. A couple boys, about 12, walked around with horses, and Amanda led Checkers, while Kerry was paired with Paloosa. The class was full with five others who trailered horses to the show.

Natalie and Kate had balanced the classes, so not all club members entered every class, and there was plenty of room for outsiders. Kazi carried herself regally, and she and Jennifer took the first blue ribbon. Mandy was happy that the little girl with the pony won second place.

There were eight entrants in the kids' classes, with Sylvia being the only club member who qualified at age 12. One small horse spooked trotting around, and the young rider fell off, uninjured, except maybe her pride. The little one with the Shetland pony won a blue ribbon in the kids' unmounted obstacle class. Each horse needed to be led calmly across a tarp, then step on an elevated wooden platform before walking between two barrels with small banners on each one.

Club members who were not participating in a certain class handed out ribbons to the riders when Natalie announced the winners. They had six ribbons for each class. Mandy sat quietly at the end of the judges' booth. She respected Natalie's riding skills and no nonsense approach to everything. She was nice and generous, but very reserved. When asked a question about her childhood or where she learned to ride or how long she had had horses, she evaded any response and changed the subject. Mandy had just met Mr. Adams yesterday at the final practice as he watched from the fence. She was very busy with show preparations and didn't have time for a conversation or anything.

In the seventh class, walk-trot any style, there was quite a commotion when one of the outsider horses riding too close behind Kazi tried to bite her. Kazi kicked at the horse behind her, then spun around to her left. Four other horses spooked slightly, and Jennifer was thrown off the horse's right side. Natalie calmly said into the microphone, "We are going to sort things out here, folks. Stay in your seats, please. Riders, pull your horses facing the closest rail, dismount, and stand where you are." She then walked to Jennifer, while the veterinarians and Colonel Paul slowly walked around the ring checking on everyone else.

Kazi was next to the fence where Mandy had been seated. She stepped into the arena and did exactly what she'd seen Colonel Paul do so often. "Easy girl, eeeeeasy Kazi," she spoke softly walking toward the white horse's shoulder. Dr. Gardner and the paramedics got to her just as Jennifer was standing up, her white "Noble Spirit Horse Club" shirt covered in dirt and her eyes brimming with tears and anger. Natalie took charge.

"Mandy, bring Kazi here, please. Jennifer, are you hurt?" She paused. "Well, if not, I will give you a leg up," she said matter-of-factly. She had lectured the girls about getting back on a horse if you fall off.

Jennifer was livid. "I am not getting on that stupid horse for anything."

Natalie was firm. "You will get on that horse, and you will do it now."

"Look at me," she practically wailed. "My shirt is all dirty, and I'm a mess."

Natalie dismissed the paramedics and her father.

"Everybody is looking at me," she weeped.

"Yes, they are, Jennifer," Natalie said without emotion. "They are looking to see how you conduct yourself in light of your little fall."

Mandy stood nearby with Kazi.

"Jennifer," she said softly. "This is the time for your 'Noble Spirit.' You have it. I know you do. You can do this. And I will admire you for it."

Jennifer flashed back to the fifth grade cafeteria where a fat boy had spilled his lunch tray, food and all. Everyone laughed and pointed, except Mandy and Emily Porter. They went to the child and comforted him, picked up everything, fixed a new tray and brought him to their table. Jennifer secretly admired Mandy from that day on. And here, Mandy was saying that she would admire her for getting back on the horse.

Jennifer gingerly put her foot out to Natalie. Mandy held tightly to Kazi's reins in front of her with both hands. Once Jennifer got her foot into the right side stirrup and was seated, Mandy put the reins over Kazi's neck and handed them to Jennifer. She could see that she was afraid.

"Breathe, Jennifer, breathe," Mandy instructed, speaking slowly. "Walk, breathe, hold the horn, walk. All the other horses are away from you. Everyone has dismounted and is standing still. Face the stands. Smile, and walk to the gate. I'll be there for you." Mandy turned Kazi toward the bleachers, then stepped away. Natalie remained standing in the ring.

The beautiful, young, now-slightly-dirtied, blond teenager gathered the reins, took a deep breath and turned the white Arabian to squarely face the stands. The spectators clapped. She spotted Mrs. Jackson smiling and waving. One of the little girls with her shouted, "Go Jennifer. We love you!" Jennifer relaxed. Mandy could see it. Then the crowd rose to their feet from one end of the bleachers to the other. Everyone cheered.

Jennifer smiled and waved. She breathed. Then she calmly turned Kazi and walked slowly to Mandy and dismounted. Big Dan opened the gate, and they left the arena. The other riders were permitted to re-mount, walking one by one back to the mounting block just inside the gate. The class proceeded with a warning about adequate spacing between horses, and Natalie thanked the riders for their timely responses in facing the horses to the fence and dismounting quickly when asked.

Carol Gardner walked over to her daughter. "Do you want me to go home and get you a clean blouse, honey?"

Jennifer looked down at her front and brushed at it again. "No, Mom, I don't think so. I'll wear this one."

"It's like your badge of the 'Noble Spirit'," Mandy said.

"I couldn't have gotten back on, Mandy, without you there," Jennifer stated. "Thanks."

"Sure, any time you fall off a horse, just give me a call!" Mandy said before skipping back to the judging booth.

"I'm very proud of you," Jennifer's mom said. "Everyone is. They were all applauding. You're really a very special young lady."

Jennifer petted Kazi's neck and looked at Carol. "And you're a special mom. I love you."

Dr. Gardner watched his wife and daughter hold a long hug. "I'm never going to lose sight of what's really important or crawl into my work so totally again," he thought to himself. "We need to share our feelings and our hurts and joys at every turn." Then he realized that he had forgotten to tell Carol that he resigned as doctor for the college football team and one of his board of directors slots.

Chapter 27

Sylvia won the youth egg and spoon event, and Mrs. White won the egg and spoon contest for everyone. The adult mounted obstacle class included walking on the tarp, over the wood platform, through the barrels and for the adult entrants, they added a curtain of Styrofoam® swimming pool noodles to walk through. Jennifer decided to watch instead of participate in any more classes, so Mandy rode Kazi, as the horse was already on the entry list.

Paloosa and Kazi were the only horses to do everything with no hesitation. The judges decided on a tie breaker. Each rider would place a plastic poncho over the horse's neck, then move it up over the head and down the face, letting it slide off, but not letting go of it from the saddle. Paloosa and Kazi both aced it. The second tie breaker was removing the banners from the barrels, waving them from the saddle, turning around, backing through the barrels and placing them back into the barrels.

As it was still a tie, and time was running out, both were awarded blue ribbons. Noble came in second. He had stopped to look more closely at the wood platform before stepping on it. Three horses wouldn't get on it, and the most of the others avoided the noodles.

The next to last class was a mounted equitation activity, where each rider is judged for position and handling of the horse at the walk and trot, as well as halting, backing up and sidepassing. Mandy was riding Paloosa in this event.

A big, black horse no one had seen yet started prancing all over once his rider mounted. Obviously, the rider couldn't slow him down. He just trotted at will, exciting a couple other horses. Before the competition even began, he jumped out of control when a large truck barreled past on State Highway 24, his rider landing with a thud and a scream and the horse heading for the gate. Two other riders fell when their horses spooked.

Big Dan scooted on the other side of the gate just as the black horse skidded to a stop a few inches away, then turned around and started trotting again all over the arena. The horses under control were facing the fence, and Natalie instructed everyone to dismount.

The girl who fell from the big horse was crying about her arm. Mandy knew what that felt like, but she had dismounted, handed Paloosa's reins to Mrs. White to hold and was busy with Kate checking on the other two riders who fell off their horses. The judges and Colonel Paul were in the ring trying to catch Apache, the big black horse and another riderless horse. Paramedics responded with an air splint and stabilized what was probably a broken limb. That girl was taken to the ambulance.

Rachel and the other fallen rider were not hurt, but shaken up too much to want to compete. The horses were caught, and all three of the thrown riders' parents were at the gate within minutes. Once the horses were turned over to their owners, and those riders were outside the ring, Natalie asked each participant to walk once around the arena before going to the mounting block. She wanted to be sure each horse was calm again.

The nine riders left included Kerry and Noble, Mrs. White and Harmony, Anne on Checkers, Razia with Sunny, one outsider and Mandy on Paloosa. Paloosa was a dream to ride, enthusiastic and totally responsive to her rider. She won the event for her third blue ribbon of the show.

The last class was the slow race. It was comical with riders trying to keep their horses moving forward as slowly as possible for the length of the arena. It looked like a tie at the end between Checkers and an unknown, buckskin horse ridden by one of the boys. He got the blue ribbon and grinned from ear to ear. "See, Mom," he yelled to a short woman standing at the fence. "I told you we could win *something!*"

As soon as the riders were out of the arena, Colonel Paul took the microphone, while Natalie and Mrs. White set up four jumps, each about two feet high. Kerry took her place at the keyboard, and Jennifer stood ready to sing once again, dirty shirt and all.

Ladies and gentlemen, we have one special grand finale for your viewing pleasure. While these young ladies here provide some very special music, Mandy Sullivan will perform on her Thoroughbred named Noble. You've seen him win several ribbons in the classes today with other riders.

Big Dan opened the gate, and Anne led Noble with Mandy on bareback while Colonel Paul continued: *Mandy is a rising sophomore in high school who has loved horses, she says, since she was 3. Noble is the first horse she has ever met or ridden, and she has been taking informal riding lessons just for two and a half months. This 20-year-old Thoroughbred is blind his right eye, leaving him with less than half sight, since horses cannot see directly in front or behind them.*

Her father closed the gate and removed Noble's halter. "Ride, sweet pea, just like you have practiced. Be safe." As Mandy walked around the arena, Colonel Paul continued. *He was picked on by other horses for his disability, and, until Cash moved here several weeks ago, Noble lived in a pasture alone – alone in all kinds of weather and darkness of night, alone from equine companionship and safety, which is very important to horses. It is his perseverance, calmness, kindness and willingness to be a friend to everyone who walks up to him that we get the Noble Spirit. It is from him that the Noble Spirit Horse Club got its name and has adopted the Noble Spirit: an inner courage that gets you through whatever life throws your way. Let's give a big welcome, a big hand, to Mandy riding her horse Noble – bareback with no bridle.*

The keyboard music began softly, and Amanda spoke again. *This song, also sung by Jennifer Nichols, is titled "The Noble Spirit." It was written by Mandy and set to music by Mrs. Engels, the music teacher at Highland Woods High School.* Kerry raised the volume and added some bass. Jennifer's voice once again rang into the air.

Mandy held tightly to Noble's mane, breathed and applied leg pressure to walk him around the arena a second time. Back by the gate, she urged him into a trot and trotted entirely around. As she cleared the gate again, she tapped him lightly with her outside leg to steer him into two jumps. He naturally picked up a canter and gracefully glided over each jump. Every jump coincided with the rise and fall of the musical notes. No one sang along. They were holding their breath. Mandy was breathing all the time. Noble was perfect.

They turned, and her gentle giant sailed effortlessly over the other two jumps, and they cantered all the way around the arena and back to the center. Jennifer sang one more chorus to the song, and the crowd gave a standing ovation that went on for five minutes. Mandy smiled and waved and walked to the gate. She leaned forward on Noble's neck and hugged him before sliding off her magnificent Thoroughbred. She put on his halter and lead rope and walked back to the judging stand with Noble where the club members had all assembled. She took the microphone.

"Thank you. Thank you. Our last award of the day is a small trophy that will be given to someone who has what we call the "Noble Spirit" – an inner grace of strength and character. It is an honor bestowed by the horse club members on a person whom they feel exhibits integrity, enthusiasm and courage. We made a list of people – and there were a lot of wonderful men and women on the list. We talked and talked and finally voted. The vote was unanimous.

The first ever Noble Spirit Award honors this lady's leadership and help organizing the horse club and this horse show, her encouragement to all of us and her steadfastness in overcoming obstacles along the path of life. She has adopted Bixlerville as her hometown, and we love her. The "Noble Spirit Award" goes to [keyboard music as close to a drum roll as a keyboard can make] ... *– Kate Dawson."*

Kate was stunned. "Stand up, Kate," Colonel Paul said.

She stood up and stepped over to the girls in the arena. The folks cheered, even though most of them didn't know her. She shyly said into the microphone: "Thank you, I am honored." She walked to each club member and hugged her through tears of joy. When she returned to her seat, she simply said, "I can't believe it." Colonel Paul leaned over and kissed her cheek. "Congratulations, Kate," he whispered.

"Now, there's enough food for two armies in back of the house at the chuckwagon and a potluck of a zillion salads and goodies. Please everyone, go and enjoy yourselves," Mandy concluded, just before a shriek from behind the house filled the air.

A Noble Spirit

Chapter
28

Pastor Porter and a few people closest to the house went running toward the sound of the scream, Dr. Gardner and the paramedics among them. Martha was standing on the deck covered in orange soda and trying seriously not to laugh. "Rosemary, Natalie's mother, didn't want orange soda and threw it at me, yelling for cream soda," she explained quickly. "I guess I screamed a bit too much when the drink and ice hit me."

Lowering her voice and turning away from the elderly woman, she explained for those who ran to her aid: "She has dementia, so she doesn't really know what she's doing much of the time. No harm done. I'll make her a cream soda."

"How?" asked Mrs. Porter, jostling one crying twin baby.

"Oh, I think I'll just put some milk in a Coca-Cola for her," Martha responded, moving toward the kitchen. She emerged a few moments later with another plastic cup, this one with ice, soda, a splash of milk and a straw.

"Here you go, one cream soda made especially for you," she said softly, approaching Rosemary from the side, so not to be in the way again of a full, flying drink cup.

"Thank you, dear. Hmmm, delicious, just what I wanted," stated Rosemary. Those gathered around nodded understandingly, all the while raising their eyebrows and rolling their eyes at the thought of the milk and soda combination.

Natalie reached her mother just as Martha was handing her the cream soda, a look of relief on her face and a grateful hug for Martha. "Thanks a lot," she said. "Go upstairs, first room on the right, and help yourself to a clean blouse; I think we're about the same size." Martha nodded and headed into the house.

Colonel Paul stayed near the barn to make sure all the farm's horses were properly tended to, and the pasture horses were put in their places. He walked around among the trailers, helping one girl load a stubborn Appaloosa, and another one get the horse trailer latches closed before her quarter horse backed out for what would have been the fourth or fifth time. Danny and his friends were doing a commendable job of managing the highway traffic and getting the trucks and trailers safely on the road.

Walking between the trailers, he bumped into a neatly dressed woman wearing an oversized straw hat, which fell off, revealing auburn wavy hair and a face that looked vaguely familiar despite the reflective sunglasses.

"Excuse me," he said quickly, retrieving the hat. "Are you okay?"

"I'm fine. I'm just leaving," she practically whispered.

"Before the picnic? There's a huge foodfest over by the house. Do you have a son or daughter in the competition? Did you come with anyone?" he asked.

She had repositioned the somewhat silly-looking straw hat with two feathers and a dried maple leaf back on her head and started to walk away when he heard Kate's voice from his left.

"Well, where do you think you are anyway? The Kentucky Derby?"

The woman stopped and turned back. In a shaky voice, she said: "I knew if you saw the hat, you'd know me, and if you didn't want to see me or talk to me, then you wouldn't approach."

Kate stepped in closer. Tears made their way down from behind the sunglasses. Kate had never seen her big sister cry, and today was the kind of day for joy and fun, not for tears or sadness.

"Hey, hey, Donna, it's okay, it's okay." Kate embraced her sister and listened to her apologies between sobs, reassuring her of her love and extreme happiness that she had driven two hours to see her and come to the horse show and chuckwagon picnic. From a small hill across the yard, Anne and Kate's mother watched the sisters' reunion and shared a high five at their joint accomplishment. Colonel Paul backed away. He wasn't needed at this little reunion.

"We've been having problems, Kate, you already knew that," Donna said. "We're seeing a counselor, and I'm staying with friends close by, so the kids are not disrupted with the new school year. We just got going the wrong way - making the little things important and the letting the important stuff get in our way. Always worrying about how we *look,* instead of who we *are.* We're going to church now, and I'm so ashamed of myself. You're family, Kate, my family, our family. You and Mom and Jimmy, Frank and Bruce and Melissa. Oh, and I went to a support group meeting for agoraphobic people. I thought they'd talk about all the things they are scared of all the time or controlling what's going on around them, but they didn't."

Kate looked puzzled. "What did they talk about?"

"Humiliation, Kate. The humiliation of the condition. How they hide it from employers, friends and even spouses; making up excuses and trying to power through situations that leave them exhausted and ashamed. I never knew, Kate ... there was a bank president, a waitress and others. Regular people. I am so sorry I didn't ... that I haven't ... I didn't know ...." She started crying again.

"It's okay, Donna, really it is. Anne and I have found our place in Bixlerille. I'm working and studying, and oh, I have so much to tell you ...I thought about calling you a couple times."

"I called you, Kate, but you didn't answer."

"I never saw a call from you. I probably wasn't at home."

"Excuse me, Mrs. Dawson," said a tall, thin man Kate had never seen. "I heard you do medical billing."

"Yes, I do," Kate replied.

"I am Dr. Jeremy Quinn of Central Pennsylvania Cardiac Associates. Call me next week if you can. I'd like to talk to you about our situation. You have been highly recommended, and we're desperate for an experienced hand," he stated, handing her a business card.

Kate assured him that she would call. She could use more work and income. Her cell phone rang, and she saw Brad's name and number. "Here, Donna, it's your husband. He must have hit the wrong button."

Donna took the phone. "Yes, yes, what? Oh. I can't believe it."

She handed the phone to Kate. "No mistake, he wants to talk to you." Kate took the phone and said "hello."

"I'm sorry, Kate, for the way we treated you. Donna and the kids miss you terribly, and I was wrong and have been mean to you. If you will forgive me, I'd like to apologize in person," he said.

Kate took a deep breath. "Okay, Brad. Thank you for calling."

"That personal apology. Uh, I'm not very good at these things. Can I do it now?" he asked.

"Well, where are you?" Kate queried.

"Right behind you."

Kate turned around to see Brad walking toward her, looking quite out of place in his casual, expensive attire. The once-perfect shine on his pricey shoes was covered in dirt and dust. He looked right in her eyes.

"I'm sorry, Kate. I apologize for what I said. I hope you have known me long enough to realize that I am not the way you saw me that day. There's been a lot of stress at home and at work, and ..."

"Okay, Brad, let's call it history."

"Good," he said smiling. "Very good." He turned and yelled. "Jimmy, Jodie, you can come see Auntie Kate now."

The twins came running from behind a white pickup truck with a classy Sundowner horse trailer behind it. Jimmy's cowboy hat fell off.

Donna was taken by surprise. Brad explained that he got a call from their mother. "She told me that Kate was going to get the trophy, and you said you were going alone, not sure what might happen. Your mom said I needed to straighten this out, and she was right. Well, we took our chances and set up this elaborate disguise. The kids came in with the Jacksons. They were bringing three children from their church, so Jimmy and Jodie just tagged along. I bought cowboy hats, kerchiefs and sunglasses for all of them, so you couldn't guess who they were or that we were all here. Anne and Mandy helped put it all together. And I rented a vehicle, even being sure it had out-of-state license plates." He turned to his sister-in-law.

"We're here for you, Kate. This is a family event, and you're the guest of honor! You deserve it."

As they walked toward the picnic, Donna asked Kate what Brad had said that was so hurtful.

The raw words stabbed afresh at her self-esteem. Kate looked at her and said, "I don't remember."

A Noble Spirit

.

Chapter
29

Colonel Paul was sauntering toward the house, realizing he was very hungry, when a couple of rising high school seniors intercepted him to ask him about going into the Army after they graduated. One of the boy's fathers joined them and suggested that, if Colonel Paul enjoyed hunting, he meet them in a few weeks to sight in their rifles before heading to a small hunting camp he owned about an hour away.

He hadn't hunted since he was a teenager and said he'd like to come along for a hunting weekend if he could get away from his work. They all got plates of barbeque, coleslaw, beans, salad and dessert and found a picnic table. They swapped hunting stories. Each of the boys had bagged his first or second deer last season and eagerly looked forward to hunting again.

At one point, Colonel Paul looked past his new friends and caught Kate's eyes. They held the gaze, an unspoken comfort and understanding flowing between them. He nodded. She smiled. His heart skipped a beat. She was so darn cute, he thought. But more than that, she was real and fun and sensitive. She smiled again before heading for the buffet. He heard that Natalie's husband had come home, but he hadn't met him yet. As he watched the crowd – familiar faces and people unknown to him, he felt - possibly for the first time in his life - that he was in a place where he belonged.

Kate and another lady were in the kitchen fixing another cream soda for Rosemary. "Is this correct?" Kate queried as she added a tablespoon of milk to the soda.

"I don't think she'll care. Thanks for doing this," Natalie said, stepping aside and gesturing Matthew forward. "Kate, this is my husband, Matthew."

Kate graciously extended her hand, "I'm very pleased to meet you. I hope you are happy here, on the ground. I know you have flown all over the world. This is my sister, Donna, from Pittsburgh. Natalie and Matthew own this farm," she explained. "The chuckwagon picnic and potluck was all her idea."

"That's a nifty little trophy, Kate. It sounds like those girls think the world of you," he said sincerely.

Natalie decided she needed to check on Rosemary and the festivities going on out back. "Come and meet the town," she said to Matthew. "I think they're all here!"

He walked directly to Rosemary, who was sipping on her second or third cream soda and knelt down to her level. "Hi Rosemary, how are you? I haven't seen you in a long time," he greeted the frail lady.

She looked at him without recognition, noted his ball cap and asked, "Do you play baseball?"

"No, ma'am," he responded. "I fly planes."

"You are wearing the wrong hat to fly an airplane," she flatly stated.

"I suppose I am," he said with an affectionate smile, patting her shoulder. "You are looking good."

"Well, I'm 75 now, and I feel good, too. How old are you?" she asked.

He happened to know that she turned 78 the previous February, but he didn't correct her. "I'm about 20 years younger than you, but not nearly as pretty."

She offered him some cream soda, which he declined, and Natalie introduced him around, leaving him with Colonel Paul and his potential hunting buddies. The boys started asking him about flying and the Air Force. He'd never been in the Air Force, he told them. He graduated from Embry-Riddle Aeronautical University in Daytona Beach. "But if you don't have the means to go there, the Air Force is definitely a good choice for flying," he stated.

Big Dan saw Sam Gardner across the yard and set out his way. "I see that your house is up for sale, and I hear you're moving to town?" he queried.

"Yes, Dan, we're moving into town. Carol is going to work at the little frame shop. She doesn't need the money, but she needs to work, if you catch my drift. Jennifer is thrilled about being near to school and friends, and she wants a horse. I was very proud of her today. I'm losing my grand house in favor of gaining back my beautiful family," the doctor conceded.

"And, Dan, that apartment addition is very, very nice. If you're going to continue in construction or renovation, I have lots of work for you. They – Carol and Jennifer – are looking at that old coal baron's mansion on the north end of Parker Avenue. It's very nice, but needs lots of updating." He winked at his buddy. "Since I'll be reducing my hours and spending more time at home, I want it brighter, more windows, and the bathrooms all need updating. Kitchen, too."

"Hey, I'll try to work you in," Big Dan said lightly. "Three people who have looked at the apartment addition here said they'll be calling for something similar. It turned out nice, the perfect in-law arrangement. You might have to 'take a number'. Looks like I'm in the construction business!"

"With your son and friend," said Danny, who had walked up behind him.

"Yes, Danny, definitely with you and Assan. I could not have done either those spreadsheets or drawings or the building without the both of you and Andy. Or the floors without Mr. Jackson. I hope you'll stay on, just part-time during school. Keep those grades up, son.

You're going to college."

Danny beamed. "And majoring in architecture! Did you see Mr. Morton sitting and laughing with the Slyders?" he asked.

Big Dan had not, but chuckled at the sight. The two men had run a wickedly bitter, mayorial campaign against one another some 15 years ago, and Mr. Morton always thought something was amiss. He didn't win, and the count difference was less than 40 votes. They hadn't spoken since. Until today.

The Noble Spirit Horse Club members sat together with people coming up to them all during the picnic. Some thanked them for having the horse show, others complimented Mandy profusely, and many patted Jennifer's shoulder and said how brave she was. The little girls with the Jacksons came to see Jennifer, who set the youngest on her lap, and everyone scooted to make room for the others on each side of her. "Whenever I fall down, I'm going to get up just like you did! You're my favorite person in the whole world," one of them said, leaning her head on Jennifer's arm.

Kate showed her mother around the barn and where the trail went up into the woods. "Mom," Kate began, "I saw Brad and Mandy's mother hug like old friends. How would they know each other? He's never been here before, has he?"

Her mom smiled. "I called him about getting this reconciliation addressed, sooner than later. Estrangement takes its toll on a person; pride steps in and paralyzes the human heart. Well, he thought of a disguise, but didn't know how to do it. He couldn't ask Donna – he didn't want her to know or try to change his mind. He couldn't call your house to talk to Anne, so he called Mandy. Martha and Brad got to talking when Mandy wasn't home. He introduced himself and told her why he and the kids needed to come 'in disguise.' They discussed different ways to do it, and he shared some of what's going on in their lives. I guess Martha is easy to talk to."

Kate nodded. "Martha is amazing."

"Most of all, Kate," she continued, "he wants to be a good husband and dad, honor God in his life and be a strong example for the kids. I told him what little I knew about Martha, how wise and knowledgeable you found her to be on life and spiritual matters.

Anyway, he called her a couple times to talk. I guess he sort of took her into his confidence. He didn't tell me much, of course - I'm his mother-in-law - mostly that Martha listened and directed him to Bible verses that matched his questions about communion and stuff. And they met today for the first time."

"So, you knew about it all along! You think they'll make it?" Kate asked.

"Oh, yes. Brad is a good, decent man who grew up very wealthy. I think he's sorting out what's meaningful. Your father used to say: 'It takes a big man to exhibit a little humility.' Donna is meeting with two ladies at their new church on dealing with anger issues and some things, too. Their love and faith will strengthen the whole family. How did you like the purple and lime green stripe in Jodie's hair?"

Kate sighed. "I hope Anne doesn't get any ideas! At least it's a temporary extension." They laughed and returned to the picnic.

Two days later, while Brad was at work and the kids were in school, Donna packed their clothes, thanked her friends for letting her and the twins stay with them and went home. She tackled dishes that were piled in the kitchen, started laundry and pulled together one of their favorite meals before jotting a congratulations e-mail to Kate for getting the cardiac doctors' new business.

The chuckwagon picnic went on for a couple hours, with people catching up with one another, meeting new folks and greeting old ones. Colonel Paul found Manuel Perez eating with his family and slipped into their conversation in Spanish. After a little while, the men the walked to the arena, and Manuel told him about the officer wanting an underground fence for his dogs.

"He said the chief's wife wants a decorative fence, too. Do you think if my brothers work those jobs with me that anyone will ask for their papers?" he queried.

"I doubt it," Colonel Paul replied. "Natalie is a lawyer, and she didn't ask for anything from you here. I don't think it's common, especially in a small town where you are getting a good reputation for quality work. And you're legal, right?"

"Sí, I am legal, mon amigo. But my brothers ... hmmm. We'll see if they call for the job, and then we can decide how to do the work.

I saw you kiss the pretty lady who got the trophy. She is the one you ride with, sí? You like her?"

"No se meta en mis asuntos," the Colonel chuckled with a warm smile.

It was close to 3:30 when men and ladies started picking up the empty dishes they had brought, rounding up kids and heading for their cars and trucks to leave. Several thanked Mrs. Adams, but most of them didn't know who owned the farm or sponsored the picnic.

Natalie and Matthew walked up a small knoll beyond the backyard and picnic area as everything was winding down. They looked at the house, arena, barn, cabin and as much of the property as they could see from there. "Welcome home, Mrs. Bixler-Adams," he said putting his arm around her shoulders. "Do they know?"

"No, no one knows. And I'm just fine with that," Natalie responded. "Just fine."

Two Boy Scout troops and a Girl Scout troop offered to clean up, so the Sullivans went home around 4:00. Martha sat at her sewing machine, studying a new pattern for a wedding dress order. She was a little behind in her work from making all the Noble Spirit Horse Club shirts, and one simply cannot be late with a wedding dress! She saw Mandy get down her backpack, put juice in a jar, and get a cookie and an apple. "You going to the hilltop today?" she asked. "School starts in the morning."

"Just for a short time," Mandy answered. Her mother watched her stuff the snacks into the pack and head out the back door.

Chapter
30

Mandy neatly laid out her aqua beach towel and looked over the farm with such happiness. It was almost picked up from the horse show and picnic, a few helpers still hauling trash bags away. She watched Colonel Paul put in the horses that belonged in stalls at night. Cash and Noble were quietly grazing in the pasture next to the woods. The other outdoor horses were standing or eating grass on the other side of the arena.

The trucks and cars and horse trailers were all gone. The rental and catering company was there, picking up the big tent, serving pots, drink containers and bleachers. She saw Mr. and Mrs. Adams walking toward the pasture where their horses grazed. They were holding hands, and everything seemed to be in its place.

She bowed her head. "Dear God," she began. "Thank you for everything. For this wonderful summer and for Noble. Thank you, God, for my family, for Colonel Paul and Mrs. Adams and my three new friends and the horse club. Help Mrs. Porter with all those children, and thank you for Mrs. Engels, and Dad's new business. If I ask you for anything, God, it's just to keep helping Mrs. Dawson get stronger and more confident. She's so sweet. And give Jennifer's parents a strong peace about her little brother. Please help me to be kind and good and a friend to everyone in school this year, even when I don't feel like it. Thank you for the 'Noble Spirit'. I love you, Jesus. Amen."

She heard leaves rustling nearby. And a crunching sound. Like the first time she saw Noble.

"Hey, hi," said Anne from behind her. "I saw you walk up. Okay if I join you? What are you doing? What are you wearing to school tomorrow?"

"Oh, you gave me a fright. The noise you made in the leaves was like the first time I saw Noble. I heard a rustling on the ground and the crunching sound of him eating, over there," she explained, pointing to the left through some low hanging branches. "Then I saw his front hooves step this way. But it's you. Sure, here, lie down." She got up and rearranged the beach towel horizontally for both of them. "I was thanking God for everything. I'm wearing dark green capris with web sandals and a white shirt that Mom put different color buttons on, probably a pink tee under."

"I want to wear my Noble Spirit Horse Club shirt, but it's not clean. Hey, we should pick a day and all wear our shirts to school! We need to make it a day when Mrs. White is subbing, too, so she can wear her red one. Well, I have lots of cool things to be thankful for. You won't laugh at me if I pray out loud, will you?" asked Anne.

"Of course not," Mandy replied.

Anne squeezed her eyes shut so tightly that Mandy almost laughed. She folded her hands tightly too, and Mandy closed her eyes.

"'Hello. My name is Anne Dawson, and I am talking to God. Thank you for moving us here. I hope we can paint the outside of our house. Thank you for helping Mom go places and for Aunt Donna, Uncle Brad and my cousins and Grandma coming to see us. Thank you for my friend Mandy and letting me show Noble and Checkers in the horse competition. That's all. Oh, wait, God. I think Mom likes

Chapter 30

Colonel Paul, and, well, I do, too. Amen.' Was that okay, do you think, Mandy?"

"I think it was beautiful, Anne. Sh-sh-sh. What's that? There can't be anything up here. I just saw Colonel Paul put away the horses, and all the others are in their pastures. There aren't any horse trailers left either. Sh-sh-sh."

Leaves were rustling nearby. They heard a crunching sound. They looked to the left. About 12 feet away, Mandy and Anne saw a front hoof step into view, then another one. They stood up as a pewter gray horse with a thick forelock and long, silver mane that fell on the right side of her neck put her head over the top rail. They walked to the fence for a closer look, knowing the horse didn't belong here. She was wearing a worn, blue halter.

They stepped up to her, and Anne grabbed Mandy's arm. "Mandy, look, there's a note taped to the halter. It says 'To Mrs. Bixler.' Who's that?

~The End~

The Noble Spirit (Song)

It's the inner courage you draw on
When you're running life's race,
[And] someone's making you unhappy.
Someone is in your face.
You think of this horse alone
Standing in a pasture half blind;
Standing tall, standing strong
Being brave, and staying kind.

When the others run him away,
He turns and walks alone.
When they bite and nip at his side,
He moves away from harm.
He holds his head up high
And looks with his one good eye.
He carries himself with pride
And relies on what's inside.

When they put you down,
You stand up tall.
When they tear you apart,
You do not fall.
Embrace your Noble Spirit
And vow to stay in the race.
And to those who try to hurt you,
Extend a measure of grace.

Tell them they can't harm you.
You're standing strong and tall.
You've got the Noble Spirit,
And you simply will not fall.
Their words cannot pierce you;
They cannot bring you down.
You have a Noble Spirit,
And that's like having a crown.

It protects your self-esteem
And keeps you safe and secure.
The Noble Spirit surrounds you,
And causes you to endure.
Move on with patience, love and joy
Peace and goodness, too.
Faith and gentleness will prevail
And you will conquer all.
With self-control in stride,
You lean on what's inside.

When they put you down,
You stand up tall.
When they tear you apart,
You do not fall.
Embrace your Noble Spirit
And vow to stay in the race.
And to those who try to hurt you,
Extend a measure of grace.

Embrace your Noble Spirit
Hold your head up high each day.
Hang tight to your Noble Spirit.
And conquer what comes your way.

When they put you down,
You stand up tall.
When they tear you apart,
You do not fall.
Embrace your Noble Spirit
And vow to stay in the race.
And to those who try to hurt you
Extend a measure of grace.